BRITTANY L.J. ROBERTS

# Catching a Match

*A Prequel to When the Flame Goes Out*

First published by WTFGO Publishing 2026

Copyright © 2026 by Brittany L.J. Roberts

All rights reserved. No part of this publication may be reproduced, stored, or transmitted in any form or by any means, electronic, mechanical, photocopying, recording, scanning, or otherwise without written permission from the publisher. It is illegal to copy this book, post it to a website, or distribute it by any other means without permission.

This novel is entirely a work of fiction. The names, characters, and incidents portrayed in it are the work of the author's imagination. Any resemblance to actual persons, living or dead, events, or localities is entirely coincidental.

Brittany L.J. Roberts asserts the moral right to be identified as the author of this work.

Brittany L.J. Roberts has no responsibility for the persistence or accuracy of URLs for external or third-party Internet Websites referred to in this publication and does not guarantee that any content on such Websites is, or will remain, accurate or appropriate.

Designations used by companies to distinguish their products are often claimed as trademarks. All brand names and product names used in this book and on its cover are trade names, service marks, trademarks, and registered trademarks of their respective owners. The publishers and the book are not associated with any product or vendor mentioned in this book. None of the companies referenced within the book have endorsed the book.

First edition

This book was professionally typeset on Reedsy.
Find out more at reedsy.com

*To my husband, Matthew. Thank you for sticking with me through all the hard parts. For better or for worse, right?*

Mania starts off fun- not sleeping for days, keeping company with your brain, which has become a wonderful computer, showing 24 TV channels all about you. That goes horribly wrong after a while.

Carrie Fisher

# Contents

*Preface* — ii
1. Baseline — 1
2. Cokes and Twizzlers — 7
3. Dungeons and Drags — 14
4. Scent-sible — 22
5. The Price of Impulse — 30
6. Driven Up a Wall — 37
7. Adios — 47
8. I'm Fine — 57
9. Audacity — 62
10. Freedom — 67
11. I Need Help — 75

Epilogue — 79
Afterword — 82
*About the Author* — 83
*Also by Brittany L.J. Roberts* — 84

# Preface

Trigger warnings: This book contains moments and mentions of the following. Reader discretion is advised.

- Misdiagnosis
- Type 1 Bipolar Disorder
- Reckless driving
- Impulse spending
- General impulsiveness
- Drug use- marijuana and alcohol
- Symptoms of psychosis, such as hallucinations, both visual and auditory
- Extreme euphoria
- Vivid descriptions of dangerous situations
- Profanity/strong language
- Disordered eating
- Child endangerment

# 1

# Baseline

It was a quiet Saturday morning. Alex, my husband, was off work, sleeping in, and I was up with Luna, our 6-year-old daughter. She was in our dining area in the living room, coloring away with her washable crayons. I was making coffee in the kitchen when my phone buzzed in my robe pocket. I knew who it was, but I really didn't want to talk with him right then. Every interaction with him felt increasingly draining. I ignored the buzz.

"Luna, do you want pancakes or cereal for breakfast?" I asked.

After a moment of silence, a high-pitched voice announced, "Cereal." I pulled a small bowl from the brown wooden cabinet in front of me, my eyes lingering on the pill bottle on top of the microwave below the cabinet. Why hadn't I thrown those meds out yet? I had stopped taking my antipsychotics with my doctor's order because of the movement disorder they caused. I felt confident in my ability to keep things under control. It had been a few months since I had stopped taking them, after all. *If I were going to have a hypomanic episode, I would have already,* I told myself confidently.

I was all too familiar with my bipolar 2 diagnosis, and I hated being so aware of it. I wished time and time again that it would have been caught years earlier, but it wasn't, even though the signs were all there. It was supposed to be the less severe version, as my hypomanic episodes never lasted more than a week, and my depressive episodes were manageable without medication.

If my father had never told me he was bipolar, I never would have connected the dots and sought help for it in the first place. That was one thing I was grateful for, at least. But why couldn't he have told me sooner? I felt like his withholding medical information from me was unfair, as I needed to know what to look out for in not only myself, but Luna as well.

After grabbing the bowl from the cabinet, I got the cereal itself off the top of the refrigerator. A brand with tons of sugar and dyes, but I didn't care. It was Saturday, and we didn't have to be health-conscious at all times. I poured the cereal and got the milk from the inside of the fridge and added that to the bowl as well. I carefully picked up the now half-full bowl and carried it out to the dining table, where Luna sat, still coloring. Placing the bowl in front of her, I walked away, pulling my phone from my pocket, mentally preparing for whatever text I might find from my father. He was probably complaining about his practically free apartment once again.

I was the result of a teenage pregnancy. After my mom found out she was pregnant with me, my parents broke up. My father was an active alcoholic at the time of my birth and didn't stop drinking for a while after. My mom kept me away from him for a long time, not convinced of his sobriety. I didn't meet him until I was in high school. At first, I was excited to finally know the man who sired me, but that quickly turned into him complaining to me about every detail of his life. He was homeless for a bit, which we couldn't help him with, and then he finally got his apartment through an outreach program, and he doesn't have to pay much of anything in terms of rent. Less than fifty bucks a month. And yet, he was still convinced a one-bedroom apartment was too small for just him. I hated how much audacity he had.

As I unlocked my phone, I saw it. The message from my father. And I was correct. He was complaining about his apartment being too small once again because his wall in the living room was too small for the flat screen he got from Craigslist for free. As if he needed a huge TV in his living room. I groaned loudly, my head tilting back and eyes on the ceiling. Did I have to reply to him? I quickly typed out a message simply stating 'that sucks,' and moved to sit on my plush brown couch. The seats were deep and comfortable. I loved that couch.

I tried to refocus my mind on what mattered most to me: Luna. She was so precious, with her shoulder-length chestnut hair and green eyes. She got her hair from Alex, and we weren't sure where the green eyes came from, as her father and I both had blue eyes, but we did have extended family with both blue and brown eyes, so maybe the genes got a little scrambled with her. Not that I was complaining. They were a beautiful shade of green.

Life with Luna wasn't always easy times and coloring pages. Luna was autistic, and with that came certain challenges. Like potty training. She wasn't fully potty trained until that year. She struggled with transitions, and she had meltdowns frequently when she was younger. Luna could also be a picky eater at times, as well as having a handful of other symptoms. But these symptoms weren't all she was.

Luna was kind and empathetic, quick to give a hug to anybody who looked sad. She was incredibly musical, having a wonderful singing voice for her age and a good sense of beat and rhythm. She loved expressing herself through her bright, colorful clothing, and her favorite color was pink. My daughter was an amazing, beautiful, and challenging little person.

I noticed she was still coloring and not touching her breakfast. If she didn't eat it soon, it was going to get soggy, and then we were going to have texture issues to deal with.

"Hey, Sweetie, it's time to eat your cereal. Can you put the crayon down, please?" I requested gently.

She hesitated for a moment, then slowly set her crayon down and swapped it for her spoon. I was expecting a full meltdown over the request, so her calmly switching tasks pleasantly surprised me, although I didn't want to show it too much and get her worked up. I kept my face expressionless, but inside, I was still struggling to let go of the text I got from my father.

"After you're done eating, would you like Mommy to color with you?" I asked her, trying to find a way to deal with the rising heat I felt.

"Okay, Mommy!" She exclaimed in her cute, high-pitched voice. She had no idea how much it grounded me to be able to play with her. Without the meds I was on previously, I had also grown more quick to anger, which isn't what it was supposed to treat, but I considered it a bonus. I just needed to learn to adjust without them. *At least I still had my ADHD medication,* I thought.

I didn't know what I would do without that, as I had a tough time focusing without it.

Just as Luna finished her food, I grabbed a crayon out of the plastic bin we kept on the table and a sheet of paper from the pile next to it. It was just a blank piece, but I loved just filling it with color. Luna mirrored my movements, pushing her bowl to the side.

"What are you gonna draw, sweetie?" I asked.

"A unicorn!" She yelled excitedly.

"Inside voice, Luna. Okay?" I reminded her. We did have neighbors.

"Okay, Mommy. I'm sorry." I hated it when she said sorry for being loud. I knew I struggled with volume regulation as well, so I felt like a huge asshole and a hypocrite when I called her on it.

"You don't need to be sorry, sweetie. We just need to use our inside voices, okay? Mommy forgets sometimes, too," I pointed out.

"Okay, Mommy," she reiterated as she drew.

I had picked up a red crayon, my favorite color, and began tracing my hand on the paper. My idea was to make a red turkey. I wasn't much of an artist, but I could do that, at least.

An hour passed of us playing together. We had switched to playing dress up, and I had a tiara on my head, pretending to be a princess having a tea party with her. I was about to get up and start doing the dishes from her breakfast when my phone rang. I quickly pulled it from my pocket and placed the tiara on the kitchen counter. It was my father. I groaned and hit the answer button as I stepped into the kitchen, quickly shifting my face into a smile and adjusting my tone to sound more cheerful.

"Hey, Dad. What's up?" I asked, not really wanting to know.

"Hey, Kiddo. I was wanting to hear from you and talk about what's been going on with me lately. How are you doing, first off?"

I knew he'd have to call and complain about it.

"I'm alright. Getting ready to go out with Luna," I lied, hoping he'd take the hint and get off the phone. He didn't.

"Oh yeah? I bet y'all are gonna go have some fun, right? I wish I were closer to you guys. I'd go with. It'd give me a chance to get out of this crappy apartment. Did I tell you the TV won't even fit on my wall? The walls here are too damn small. I swear I need a bigger place."

That man knew exactly how to put me on edge. I felt my jaw twinge, and my chest became tight with unspoken annoyance. I wanted to say something, but I gritted my teeth and bore it.

"Yeah, you mentioned it before, Dad. I really have to get going. I'll call you later, okay? I love you."

"Hang on, there's something else I wanted to talk to you about. Your sister won't answer me. I swear, Lily has nothing going on ever. Why won't she make time for me?"

"Dad, I really have to go. I don't know why she won't talk to you," I said, wanting the conversation to be over.

"She's so freaking stupid, you know?"

I paused. Did he seriously insult Lily? He's never done so before. He's bragged about the nature of my and his relationship, talking about how I just got him better than her, and I tried to brush it off, but this? After he abandoned her when she was a baby because being her father was "too much?" That was my breaking point. Lily and I didn't have a relationship, but I was not going to take him insulting her lying down.

"Excuse me?" I asked, the fury not yet clear in my voice.

"Yeah, I mean, I'm her father. She should want to talk with me. I want to talk with her. You talk to me. Why can't she? Little dumbass," he said with vitriol in his voice.

"Fuck you," I said, my tone laced with ice.

"What did you just say to me?" He asked, sounding offended.

"Fuck you. You abandoned her, and you expect her to be grateful? Pull your head out of your ass. Never contact me again. I'm done," I said and hung up. I proceeded to pull up his number and block it before he could call again, doing the same with his email address so he couldn't try to email me either. That was the straw that broke the camel's back. He would not insult his own child to me.

My internal bullshit tolerance meter was about to boil over, and it was going to be ugly. I needed to get out of there, but I couldn't let Luna see that. Stalking into the bedroom, I found Alex still asleep in bed. I shook him awake as gently as I could manage and told him I needed him to watch Luna. I needed a break.

He got up almost immediately, recognizing the ice in my tone.

"Are you okay?" He asked, his long chestnut hair falling around his shoulders. His hair was one of my favorite things about him.

"I will be. Can you please stay with Luna for a bit? I think I need to take a drive. Clear my head. It was my dad. I'm done. I'll explain more later," I said, changing my clothes quickly and reaching for the car keys on the table next to Alex.

"Hold on, are you gonna be safe on the road? You seem pissed."

"I'll be fine. I'm just gonna go for a drive, maybe pick up some treats for us while I'm out," I said, trying to make my voice sound less angry. "I promise not to intentionally kill anyone, okay?"

"It's the unintentional I'm worried about. Go take a drive, but please, be careful," he said, making it clear that was the caveat to my leaving.

"I will be. Love you." I quickly left the room and headed out the front door towards my car.

# 2

# Cokes and Twizzlers

As I approached the car, I felt ready to punch through a wall. I unlocked the door manually with the key, the electronic fob needing a new battery. I opened the door hard and climbed in, slamming it shut, not caring who saw.

How the hell did he expect me to react when he was actively insulting his other kid, my sister? Did he think just because we didn't have much of a relationship that I'd be okay with him insulting her? How stupid was he? I pulled out of the parking spot we had on the side of the street quickly, my movements deliberate and harsh. Blasting some music from my "Break Shit" playlist sped down the road, going five, then ten miles over the speed limit, daring somebody to pull me over. I knew what I was doing was illegal and a little dangerous, but I didn't care. I just needed to go. Where, I wasn't sure. I just needed to move and fast.

The raw scream in my throat bubbled over, all while I was speeding down the road. The music was loud enough to almost drown out the sound of my unfiltered voice. I probably looked completely nuts, but I didn't care. I needed to let it all out. My throat became hoarse, demanding a drink of water. Or soda, as my cravings told me.

I pulled over into a gas station I knew was about 10 minutes away from my apartment. It wasn't far, but I had driven there fast. I pulled into the parking spot quickly, exiting the car swiftly, slamming the door shut once again. Inside the small station, I got a water bottle, sodas, and a Sprite for

Luna. I didn't want her to experience caffeine addiction, like I did. As I paid at the counter, I saw the cashier's demeanor change. He shifted his weight a few times, avoiding my gaze, hurriedly getting my items scanned and put into a bag. He didn't ask how my day was, but politely told me my total. I yanked my card from my wallet to pay and replaced it once I received confirmation from the card reader that my payment had gone through.

I grabbed my bag without thanking the cashier, realizing I had made him anxious, but the majority of me didn't care. The anger had started to wane, but I still had pent-up energy. That small bit of adrenaline coursing through my veins. Maybe a few more minutes out of the apartment would do me some good. Luna and Alex didn't need to see all this, I thought.

After a few more minutes sitting in the car alone in the parking spot, I made the short drive home, not speeding as much; however, I did run a red light, barely. It was solidly red, but nobody else was coming, and I was sick of being stagnant. Luckily, nobody was around to see it. I figured just that once wouldn't be an issue. I knew there were no cameras at that intersection, so I had just gotten off Scot-free.

I pulled into my spot on the side of the street in front of my apartment building. Taking a deep breath, I checked my reflection in the mirror, making sure my face didn't betray me. I looked relatively normal aside from my pupils being big, which I attributed to the adrenaline from earlier, on top of running the red light.

I got out of the door and shut it normally. As I walked to the apartment, bag of beverages in hand, I wondered if Alex and Luna were worried about me. I knew Alex saw the anger, but I didn't know if Luna had. I didn't want her to. She might've seen it as I was leaving, but at least it wasn't directed at her. Maybe I could suggest we go out and do something fun together. We hadn't done so in a while. Not since the beginning of summer before Luna started first grade. It was now solidly Autumn. Well past time to go out and have fun as a family. I walked in the door and saw Alex and Luna playing together in the living room. I couldn't tell what the game was, but it looked fun. Alex had a cape on, and Luna wore a princess dress from her toy box.

"Hey, guys. How about we go to that indoor playground? We haven't been in forever," I suggested. I really wanted to still be out and about, not ready to be home, but not wanting to be alone either.

Alex gave me a look. I'd normally talk through ideas regarding going out as a family before announcing them in front of Luna, but I wanted to be spontaneous. I wanted some wholesome family fun.

"What?" I asked him defensively.

"We're supposed to be saving money, not spending it. Luna's birthday is in a month. We need the money for the venue," he stated.

"I know, but it's just one day, and it's not like it's going to be over a few bucks for entry anyway," I said in my most convincing voice.

Alex sighed. A reserved sound. I knew all I had to do was phrase it like that, and he'd see my point. I wanted to go out, and I wanted him and Luna to be with me and have some fun. A welcome distraction from the phone call with my father.

"Playground?" I heard Luna ask, her little face lit up at the mention of it. If Alex said no, then he was gonna look like the bad guy to Luna.

He looked between her and me and finally conceded.

"Yes, sweetie. We're going to the playground," Alex said to her.

"Yay! Playground!" She yelled as she jumped up and down with joy.

"Inside voice, Lulu," Alex reminded her. I stood there, arms crossed, a satisfied smirk on my face.

"Go get dressed. We'll leave as soon as you're ready, sweetie," I told her, smiling.

As Luna ran to her room, supposedly to get dressed, Alex cornered me.

"Brina, we can't be doing this all the time, okay? We need to talk things out alone and not in front of Luna when you want to take us out as a family. I thought we were in agreement," he chided.

I immediately felt defensive. There I was trying to do something fun for the three of us, and he was getting on to me? Why? I didn't get it. It's not like the indoor playground was all that expensive.

"Alex, it's one day. I promise to talk with you ahead of time before I announce plans to Luna, but can you let it go and just have some fun for once? Please? For me?" I asked pleadingly. I didn't want him to ruin this outing with his negativity.

"Yeah, we can do it today. No more, though, alright? Anyway, what exactly happened on that call? You said you were done. What does that mean? What did he do this time?" He inquired.

"He insulted Lily. Called her stupid. I couldn't let that stand. I'm done with him. He's given me no choice but to go no contact. I can't do it anymore. All the whining and bitching when he's literally getting everything for practically no effort. I can't. I just can't," I lamented.

"He seriously called Lily stupid? I never did like your father. I'm sorry you had to deal with all that, Hun. Come here," Alex said as he wrapped his arms around me in a bear hug.

I squeezed him back and stood there for a minute, letting the warmth from his body envelop and comfort me.

***

The ride to the indoor playground was about half an hour long. Alex was driving. The air in the car was light and playful, with Alex and me singing along to a popular song on the radio and Luna playfully demanding that we stop, so naturally we only sang louder, much to her feigned disapproval. It was a lot of fun.

When we'd finally arrived at the playground, we saw it was absolutely packed. Cars filled the parking lot with few vacancies. Luna would have the chance to meet lots of new friends. We parked, and I hurried around to Luna's door to get her out of her booster seat, as she still struggled with the buttons involved and pressing them with enough pressure to trigger the latch.

I quickly and expertly undid the booster seat, and Luna got herself out of the car. She was bouncing up and down, cheering "Playground! Playground!" while I grabbed her hand and Alex her other. We swung her between us every few steps and she giggled with each turn.

"I wanna go play!" Luna exclaimed as we entered the large building, entirely dedicated to little kids and their varying abilities. She made a beeline for the ball pit as Alex went to pay for the three of us.

Inside the playground, there was the ball pit that Luna ran to, several slides along the walls, a jungle gym, and a handful of sensory centers where the kids could play with specialty textures. All this was on top of a foam-like floor, so it was soft enough that if a kid fell, they wouldn't get seriously hurt.

Alex returned to us with wristbands in hand, two green, which I assumed were for him and me, and a pink one for Luna. They all had two hours' time ahead of us written on them. I guessed he only paid for that instead of the whole day. I got my wristband from Alex and secured it on my left wrist, and then helped Luna put on her pink one. Lucky for her, it was her favorite color, so that should've eliminated any sensory issues that might've come with wearing a bracelet.

I let Luna run into the ball pit once her wristband was secured. I turned to Alex and smiled triumphantly. "See? She's having a blast," I pointed out. Luna was busy throwing colorful balls within the confines of the ball pit. She was giggling and throwing herself all around. The picture of glee and happiness.

"Okay, fine, you're right. This was a good idea, but we can't do this too often. We're still supposed to be saving, alright?" Alex reiterated.

I sighed and rolled my eyes. Of course, he had to be Mr. Practical even when we were supposed to be out having fun with our daughter.

"Fine, Alex. I get the message. But can you cheer up and join me in playing with Luna?" I said as I started to run for the ball pit myself, looking to end that conversation. It felt like he was beating a dead horse. We already agreed to be cautious with money before we left the house. I didn't know why he was bringing it up again.

I lept into the ball pit with Luna, tackling her gently, a shriek and giggles following. I started grabbing balls and trying to bury her with them. She kept throwing them off while laughing wildly. My own laughter echoed hers.

I was getting looks from the other parents and guardians in the playground, and the adults started pulling their children away from us, but I didn't care. I was having innocent fun with my little girl. So what if I matched her boundless energy? It only meant she had a super-involved mother who actually enjoys playing with her. I didn't care if I looked out of place. All I cared about was giving Luna a good time.

Alex even started to look a bit sheepish and left us to go and sit at a nearby empty table. I wanted to call out to him and ask him to join us, but an influx of children in the ball pit stopped me. They all wanted the one grown-up in there to bury them, like I had with my own daughter. I decided against it and moved to leave the pit, leaving Luna with a group of potential new friends.

I was breathless and panting, probably red-faced as well. I walked over to Alex, smiling like mad. "You've gotta get in there with her at some point. That's so much fun!" I exclaimed.

"No, thanks, I think I'm good," Alex said, his face still pink with embarrassment.

I looked at him, heat building in the pit of my stomach. "What? Are you embarrassed to have a wife who actually plays with her child?" I asked, getting directly to the point.

"No, it's not that I'm embarrassed of you playing with Luna. It's how you were playing with her. You were so loud and acting like a kid yourself. Can you rein it in a bit, Honey?" He requested.

I couldn't believe he was asking that of me. We were at a playground, for fuck's sake. A place meant for loud sounds and play. It didn't matter that it came from an adult. It was someone just having fun. Why would that be embarrassing?

"I'll try," I said through gritted teeth. "I'm going to get a drink from the little store in here. Watch Luna." I stalked off, my body internally vibrating with unspent energy. I knew it would be wise of me to take a moment so I wouldn't blow up at Alex in a public place. It was over something so small, too. Why didn't he get that I was having fun with our daughter?

I looked around the little store inside the playground. It had plenty of snack and drink options. I decided to get 2 Cokes, one for Alex as well, regardless of the fact that he had pissed me off. He was still my husband and friend. I also saw a juice box and got that for Luna. I looked around at the snack section and decided to get some cotton candy and Twizzlers, and went to check out. The cashier who rang me up looked like she couldn't have been older than 16. She told me my total. It was over twenty dollars, which felt like a lot, but I didn't care. I just wanted to get some drinks and sweets for my family. To hell with the price.

The frustration that had been there before had settled as I walked to rejoin

Alex, our treats and drinks in hand. I beamed at him as I handed him his Coke and Twizzlers, knowing that would perk him up. Alex had always been a snacker. This was the easiest way to get him to forget a disagreement.

# 3

# Dungeons and Drags

A little more than a week had passed since going to the indoor playground. I'd been a bit energetic, but that was brushed off as me just being in a good mood. I'd been working on a Dungeons & Dragons campaign for Alex to play. He was normally the dungeon master and never really got to play, so I figured I could take a turn. It had become an all-consuming project, as I'd never DM'd before. I was researching gameplay and special combat rules. I really went all out planning a whole world for him. It was a lot. All the non-player characters had backstories that were pretty elaborate. A coming-of-age ritual was integrated into the game that I wanted the player character to participate in as a way to stop being seen as an outsider. I had so much planned out.

I hadn't noticed when I started neglecting household chores, like getting dishes and laundry washed, but Alex certainly did, and he wasn't happy about it.

"Hun, I appreciate you working so diligently to write a campaign for me, but I still need you to pull your weight with chores, okay?" He said one night after Luna was asleep in bed.

I looked at him, a small pit of irritation forming in my stomach. "I'll try, but Alex, you realize I've never been the dungeon master before, right? It takes a lot to do that when my knowledge of the game as a whole is pretty damned minimal," I pointed out with exasperation. Couldn't he understand at least that? The dishes would still be there for me to do when I was finished writing out the campaign.

"I get that, Honey, I do, but I work full time. You don't. I really can't pull our weight with the household chores. It's just not feasible," he added, trying to show me the logic behind his statement.

I could feel the pit in my stomach growing, but I knew he was right, so I agreed with him begrudgingly. He sighed. A sound of relief. I huffed slightly and walked to the kitchen to start doing the pile of dishes I'd been neglecting. It was true. He couldn't do all the chores for both of us. I was a stay-at-home mom, and our daughter had even started 1st grade. I definitely needed to be the main one doing the chores at home. It wasn't like I had to go and work as Alex did. I had no demands during the day on weekdays other than chores, so I really didn't have any excuse for them not to be done.

The pile of dishes wasn't too high, but it was still daunting. *Just fucking do it. It's not that hard,* I told myself harshly. I turned on the hot water, put on my dishwashing gloves, and went to work. It wasn't that doing the dishes was difficult; it was more of the fact that they weren't interesting. If something didn't hold my interest, it often got neglected. Probably why I had so many failed relationships in the past. At least, that had to be part of it, right?

Before Alex, I had a few tumultuous relationships with men who were not good for me. I dated older guys before, thinking that would mean that they were more mature than the guys my age. I couldn't have been more wrong. They ended up being some of the biggest babies I'd ever met. I often ended relationships due to them growing stale. I'd get bored, tired of being offered the same things over and over again. Or, rather, not being offered enough. Until Alex, that was. He offered me the bit of spontaneity that I needed in my life. But that was before we became parents. Now, he had to be practical and responsible. I did, too, but it was more of a challenge for me.

The pile of dishes had grown smaller and smaller as I thought until they were done. I had all the newly cleaned dishes stacked in the drying rack to the right of me on the counter. I felt a sense of pride, of accomplishment. Happy that they were finally done, and now I'd have Alex off my back for the rest of the day, so that I could focus solely on the campaign.

I returned to the living room, that sense of accomplishment clear on my face.

Alex gave me a smile, and I took my seat by his side, the anger from earlier gone. It got worked out while I was doing the dishes, taking all of it out on the food waste that remained on them. I cuddled into his side, and he wrapped his arm around my waist.

"What do you wanna watch tonight, my love?" He asked me, the remote in his right hand, poised to click any button I commanded.

"Why don't we pick up that one anime again? I can't remember what it was called, though. Something with a cellphone in the title," I suggested. He normally knew what show I was talking about. A little thing he's learned to do in the years we'd been married. Picking up on my nonspecific wants and desires, and then translating them in his brain. He was an incredibly attentive partner. He knew all my restaurant orders to the T. He even knew what I'd probably like at any new restaurants we got to try. I'd become a bit reliant on him to tell me what he'd think I'd like, not unable to make my own decisions, but rather, trusting his judgment. It wasn't just TV and food that he knew about me. It was nearly everything. He knew me better than I knew myself.

"I know the one. I think we were watching it on my profile," he said as he got the anime pulled up.

He had no idea how grateful I was for him. I don't think I could've married a better man. As a partner, I felt like I paled in comparison. I didn't have all his restaurant orders memorized as he did for me. Instead, I had them written down in my phone under his contact name. What I did have memorized were his measurements. I knew what size clothes to get him when I did occasionally go shopping for him. Knowing all three of our measurements, I was the one assigned to purchase clothing for everyone in our household. I suppose that made up for not memorizing his food orders.

I looked at the shirt Alex was wearing. It was a dark grey graphic T-shirt that he had owned since high school. I wondered if his style would ever change, but I wouldn't mind one way or the other. He tended to dress very comfortably and casually. I tried to do the same, but my clothes were often 'extra', according to Alex. I also wore a lot of black in general. Seeing me in a color other than black was considered a rare treat for the discerning friend or family member.

As I was pondering clothes, Alex got the anime loaded up and hit play. I was hardly paying attention, my mind still on his clothes. I wanted to get him a new shirt. Something that would be a new favorite. But what? A shirt with logo from one of the shows he liked? Maybe. It was certainly an option. I pulled out my phone and began to search for men's graphic T-shirts, filtering the results for things I knew Alex liked.

As I was scrolling, I forgot Alex's presence next to me. I was so absorbed in my search for the perfect shirt.

"Distractable tonight, are we?" He asked jokingly. When he spoke, I nearly jumped out of my skin.

Once my heart was firmly back in my chest, I showed him my phone. On the screen was a list of results from one of his favorite movies of all time, How to Train Your Dragon. There were shirts for all the characters and dragons.

"I wanted to get you a new T-shirt. I know you love this movie, but you don't really have any merch from it. Figured you could use a new shirt, anyway. This one is starting to fray at the edges," I said as I gently tugged on his frayed sleeve cuff.

"Hun, as much as I appreciate how thoughtful you are, we can't right now. Luna's birthday is in less than a month. After it's over, we can look into this again. When we have more money. Okay?" He pleaded.

I was spending a little bit more than normal, and the snacks at the playground the other day put us slightly over budget, but not by much. However, it was enough to trigger another disagreement with Alex. This most recent chiding over my impulsive spending made me defensive once more.

"Who said I was trying to buy it now? I know we have to save. I was only looking," I lied, hoping it was convincing.

"Uh-huh. Well, I'll give you the benefit of the doubt. Save that one, with the dragons all together. I like it," he stated, giving me some leeway.

I took a screenshot of the shirt he wanted and kept it saved on my phone. Little did he know I'd buy it later. I really wanted to get him a present. He could be mad in the moment. I knew he'd thank me later. It wasn't like it was crazy expensive, either. Only about twenty-five bucks or so with tax. It wouldn't be enough to interfere with our bills or getting Luna's birthday presents paid for. I didn't think I was forgetting any bills. I resolved to buy the shirt once Alex had forgotten this conversation.

The hours passed quickly as I cuddled with my husband, watching the same anime on TV instead of going to bed. It was late. Already past midnight. I really should've been tired but I wasn't. Actually, I had a fair amount of energy. I wanted to work on the D&D campaign, but Alex had put a stop to that for the night when I nearly missed Luna's bedtime routine because I was so involved in it. He began to yawn, and I knew time was running out until he suggested we went to bed. I wasn't going to be able to sleep, but I could get more cuddles from Alex until he was asleep, and then leave the room. It was a solid plan.

"I think it's nearly time for bed, Brina. I'm getting tired. What about you?" He asked me.

"I'm not tired yet," I told him truthfully. "But I'll happily give you cuddles tonight."

He smiled at that. A small concession on my part, but not an unwelcome one. "I'd like that." I felt a pang of guilt hit my chest, knowing I was planning to get back up after he was asleep. I felt like part of me was abandoning him, or at least our routine.

"After this episode, we can head to bed," I stated, feigning interest in the anime. I just wanted to see if I could start to try and feel tired. I knew if I tried to lay down to sleep right then, it would be a fruitless effort.

"Okay, deal. Thanks for not putting up a fight," he stated simply.

*Put up a fight? I normally don't. What is he talking about?* I wondered. I wanted to question him on it, feeling defensive.

"What do you mean by that? I didn't think I normally put up a fight," I questioned, a bit annoyed, but mostly confused.

"Well, you normally fall asleep out here on the couch and then fight me about moving to the bedroom. Or do you not remember those nights? You're usually pretty out by the time I tell you it's time for bed. You whine at me," he teased.

"I do not whine," I whined at him.

"Like that? You kinda do, Love. Sorry." He held up his hands, showing he meant no offense by his statement.

"You're all good, Alex. I just don't like getting called out. You know that, though," I pointed out.

"You need to be called out sometimes, Hun."

That did it. I felt the hairs on my arms stand straight up, and I had no chance of physically stopping myself from giving him a piece of my mind. His words went straight to the fiery pit of anger that I had been suppressing.

"That's rude. You don't just call people out if what they're doing isn't hurting anyone," I stated, my tone clipped and short.

"I'm sorry, but it's true, Brina. You know it."

"Don't tell me what I know," I replied, feeling the heat of my anger start to spread. There was no backing down, and Alex was my target. Why did he have to push me? Why'd he start this fight? He couldn't have just let it go. He had to ruin a perfectly good evening by picking on me.

"Hun, I already said I was sorry. What else do you want?"

"Oh, really? 'I'm sorry, but,' isn't an apology. It's you trying to cover your ass," I spat out, my tone laced with ice.

"You're right. I'm sorry. Please, forgive me. I wasn't trying to upset you. I don't want to fight," he said, pleadingly. I could see the emotion in his eyes, telling me he meant every syllable. But that didn't mean I was automatically not angry with him anymore. I needed space.

"Alex, I'm taking a bathroom break. Go to bed, I'll join you when I'm done," I stated, not accepting nor rejecting his apology. Before he could reply, I'd pulled myself away from him and stood up. I walked to the bathroom, nearly stomping. I went in and shut the door, locking it behind me, not wanting him to follow me. What I needed was to cool down. I wanted to smoke some weed. I looked around for the hiding space we kept it in, on top of the highest shelf in our linen cabinet, behind a folded pile of towels. As I stood on my tiptoes to reach it, cursing my short stature, I nearly knocked the pile to the floor. I finally got the shoebox out from behind the towels. I opened it up, and inside was exactly what I wanted. Weed.

*Hell, it might even help me get some sleep*, I justified to myself. I packed a bowl of the strong-smelling pre-ground flower and pulled a red lighter from the back of the box. I didn't know why I felt like I was sneaking around. Alex knew about my weed use. He smoked it, too, on occasion. I just smoked it more frequently than him. And it had grown even more common. I summed it up to the extra stress from that phone call with my father.

I lit up the bowl and took a deep drag from the handheld pipe. I held it for a moment before releasing the smoke carefully, not wanting to start coughing, but I wanted that all too familiar light feeling that I knew would help me get to sleep and calm down from my fight with Alex. I continued to smoke more and more until the bowl contained nothing but ash. I was feeling good, and a look in the mirror confirmed what I already knew. I was high, and it showed on my face. My eyelids were heavy, and the whites of my eyes were red, but my mind still raced. My thoughts then felt like a constant onslaught, determined to claw their way out of my head. I knew Alex wouldn't get onto me for this, but he might for leaving in the middle of an argument. But it was either this or he was going to get yelled at.

I turned on the overhead fan with the switch by the door, sprayed myself down with body spray, and left the bathroom quickly, looking to see if Alex had listened to me and gone to bed or if he lingered in the living room. He wasn't there, so I assumed he went to bed. I immediately moved to the bedroom, opening the door quietly and entering before closing it shut again. I was in the bathroom for maybe 10 minutes, so he was probably still awake. Turning my head, I looked at the bed in the center of my room where my husband lay waiting for me. I couldn't make out his expression in the darkness.

"Hi, Honey," I said rather sheepishly, embarrassed over my storming out earlier.

"Yes, you are. High that is," he replied shortly. I guess my leaving so abruptly to go smoke left him in a bad mood. I should've known. How could I not? *Stupid*, I kicked myself mentally.

"I'm sorry for storming off. I do forgive you for getting onto me. Can I join you?" I requested.

Alex sighed and lifted a corner of the comforter, signaling that it was okay for me to join him in the bed. I moved quickly and got cuddled up next to him, letting the comforter fall cozily around me. I suddenly felt drained. Not sleepy exactly, but worn out despite my brain still being on overdrive.

Alex pulled me closer to him and pressed a kiss to the back of my head.

"I love you. Can you promise me this won't become a regular thing?" He requested. I didn't know what he meant. The arguments or the weed.

"I love you too. What do you mean?" I asked for clarification.

"All of this. You arguing with me, storming off, smoking weed. All of it. I need you. Luna needs you," he said, stroking my hair with his fingers.

I felt the gravitational pull towards his arms increase. I wasn't going to fight it. Why was I so quick to anger and argue with Alex lately? I could normally keep my anger under wraps, but it's been different lately. However, I had no intention of it becoming the norm. And as far as the weed went? That was only meant to be occasional. That night was an occasion. Albeit not a good one.

"I promise," I said as I snuggled closer to him. I closed my eyes and tried to will my brain to shut down.

Alex was soon snoring next to me, and my head was still switched on. I might've been physically tired, but my mind was not ready to let me sleep. Letting out a quiet sigh, I disentangled myself from Alex and went to the living room, where the D&D books were stacked on top of the coffee table. I figured if I couldn't sleep, I might as well be productive. I grabbed a book and got to work expanding my plans for the campaign until I saw the first light of day. *Crap. Alex is going to be pissed*, I thought.

# 4

# Scent-sible

Alex had gotten Luna up and ready for school. I was slightly more tired than before, but the high from the weed was gone. I wished Luna well before the pair of them left the apartment. I knew I was in for a lecture when Alex got back, by the look on his face when he saw me with the D&D books surrounding me this morning. He looked so defeated. Not angry, just fed up. He told me to go to bed, and I did without question.

As I lay in my bed, I noticed how big it felt without Alex in it. How cold and empty it was. I ran my arm over his spot. I needed to get it together because I had responsibilities I needed to take care of. Promising myself not to argue with Alex when he got home. I'd hear him out and try to do better. I didn't know what was up with me lately. Sleeping during the day was something I hated doing. I even hated naps. Daytime was meant for productivity, not sleep. I sat up in bed, unable to rest, so I remained there and waited. We lived close to the school, so Alex should've been back in about 10 minutes, give or take.

I wasn't going to say anything. Whatever he requested of me, I'd do it. Or not do it. I didn't know what he was going to say. I only knew I was going to be ready to hear it.

I heard the car pull up outside, the familiar knock of the loose bumper alerting me to its presence. I heard the car door open and then shut. Hard. *Shit.* He was angry. But it was my own fault. I was going to have to get through whatever he had to say to me.

The front door opened, and I waited for it to close harshly, but he didn't slam the door. Maybe he wasn't that mad. I still didn't want to move. Not ready to face his ire. I heard his footsteps, normally very light, fall heavily as they got closer to our bedroom door. It fell silent. I held my breath, waiting for the door to fly open. For him to launch into a tirade about how irresponsible I'd grown, to say something along the lines of him being disappointed in me. But it didn't happen. The door didn't open, and then the footsteps walked away. I guessed he thought I was asleep. Not like I could.

I knew it was nearly time for him to get ready for work, so I got up from the bed, dressed in day clothes, and headed out of the bedroom door, going to let him know I was awake still and ready for the day. *What was a single day of missed sleep?* I rationalized. I walked into the living room and sat on the couch, ready to listen if Alex had anything to say to me. He wasn't there. Maybe he was in the bathroom? Or the kitchen? I got up and checked the kitchen to find him preparing a sandwich. Something I'd normally do for him. He didn't look at me or acknowledge my presence in any way. He just kept making his PB&J.

"I'm sorry, Hun. I couldn't sleep," I said in an effort to break the awkward silence. His face softened a bit, but he continued to wordlessly make his lunch. He moved from one end of the kitchen to the other, moving to leave and go to the living room, but I was in his way. He sighed. I wasn't going to let him through until he acknowledged me.

"You promised only last night to start trying to do better. And then you stayed up all night working on the D&D campaign. And even worse, you're still up! Can't you try to sleep?" He asked rather loudly. I jumped a bit, but didn't move otherwise. He saw this, and his face softened even further. It bothered him a lot when I jumped if he was being loud. I couldn't help it. Loud, sudden noises scared me. But I figured that was normal. Who wouldn't jump at an unexpected noise aimed in their general direction?

"Sorry, I didn't mean to say it like that. It's just... Brina, you know I love you with my whole heart, so it deeply concerns me when I see you start to lose sleep over a project. And then the whole deal with your storming off last night? What was that about? You know we talk things through. What's going on in your head, Hun?" He asked pleadingly. His face was full of concern, not anger.

I thought, really thought, about what was going on with me lately. I genuinely didn't know. Maybe it was all the extra stress from going no contact with my dad, and I needed a distraction?

"I think it's because of my dad. He really got to me. I've been throwing myself into the campaign so I could try to avoid thinking about him. How can you call your own child stupid? I realize he wasn't speaking about me, and I don't have much of a relationship with Lily, but still. Who does that?" It really had been weighing on me. I hadn't really considered why I was so into planning this campaign, but this made the most sense.

Alex's shoulders relaxed some, and he embraced me, holding me close. "I'm sorry, Hun. I hadn't even considered that. Maybe it's time for you to go back to therapy. Work out this 'no contact' stuff. But I still need you to try, okay? Try to do better for Luna and me," he requested of me once more.

"I will. I'm gonna try, Alex. I'll get back on top of chores, and I'll try to back off the campaign some," I promised, fully intending to follow through on it. A lot of hours were spent working on that campaign. However, I wished he knew how much I wanted to get it planned out for him. This campaign was supposed to be a gift to Alex. I genuinely wondered why it was a bad thing that I was putting so much time into it. I knew it was a lot of time, but it was going to be so worth it in the end. He was going to love the coming-of-age ritual I included.

"And I want you to promise me that you won't smoke weed every night, alright? I know I can't stop you, but I don't want it to turn into a crutch. I understood last night, but please back off on it."

I didn't know why, but that struck a small chord with me. Did he think I was going to get addicted? I'd smoked off and on for years and hadn't been addicted or dependent on it. Why was it bothering him now?

"I promise it won't be every night. Why are you so worried? It's just weed," I asked, crossing my arms. Of all the substances I could consume, weed was probably the safest. That included caffeine. Which I actually was addicted to. I knew people joked about being addicted to it, but I got real withdrawal symptoms the one time I tried to quit drinking soda and coffee cold turkey. It was awful. Worst headache of my life. I ended up in the hospital over it. They had to give me a migraine cocktail; it was so bad. Alex was there for that. He saw how I got so snippy and pissy with everyone around me when I'd stopped. It wasn't good.

"I just don't want you using it as a crutch. That's it. I know things with your dad are raw right now. I get it, I really do. But I don't want you losing yourself to something just to avoid thinking about him and what he did. Does that make sense?"

It did make a lot of sense. I knew what he meant. I was going to back off the weed, even though it had only been twice that I had smoked this week. Maybe that was still too much for his liking.

"It makes sense, Hun. I get where you're coming from. I'll back off on it some. But I don't promise to stop entirely, fair?" I said, introducing my own caveat, giving him a wry smile.

"That's fair. I wasn't asking for you to stop entirely. Just slow down. Listen, Brina, I've gotta leave for work, but we can talk more when I get home tonight. I love you. Try to have a good day, okay?" He said as he pressed his lips to my forehead, kissing me goodbye.

"I will try," I offered. "I love you, too, and I hope you have a good day at work."

I moved to let Alex step out of our small kitchen and out the front door. He turned as he left and gave me a final smile before closing the front door. I had the whole day to myself. Dishes were finished from the night before, as none of us were breakfast people, except for Luna, who ate at school with her friends. Of course, on weekends, Alex and I would take turns getting up early to make breakfast for her, but neither of us really ate at that time. So, it didn't strike me as odd when I didn't feel hungry that morning.

What was I going to do while I waited for Alex and Luna to come home? Laundry? No, Alex did it over the weekend, and we only had enough built-up dirty clothes for a quarter-sized load, so that would be wasteful.

My mind wandered and landed back on the campaign. I knew I told Alex I'd back off, but the chores were already done. I had nothing else to do that day until Luna got off the bus at 3 o'clock.

Nope. I promised Alex that I'd back off. Time to switch objectives. What could I find to do that would effectively let me burn off some energy and be productive at the same time? I went to the kitchen to look around. Our pantry was looking a bit bare. As was our fridge. Alex didn't want me spending unnecessary money, but groceries were necessities. I pulled my phone from my jeans pocket and loaded up my grocery store app, ready to do some online shopping. Although not the fun kind. I hated going to the actual grocery store to shop. It was loud and bright. The fluorescent lights were too blue-tinted, and the music they played sounded too tinny over the intercom system. People were often in the way or were being overly obnoxious. It was a sensory assault. I'd much rather order my groceries from the comfort of my own home and then quickly pick them up than go in-store. I would've opted for delivery, but Alex wouldn't swing the few dollars it would cost to have them delivered.

I loaded up my virtual cart with loads of lunch and dinner options as well as a few snack foods. Balance was key. If I didn't keep sweets stocked up in the house, Alex would pout. That was one extra expenditure he didn't mind. That man had a sweeter tooth than anybody else I'd ever met.

An ad flashed across my screen as I went to check out. It was for the exact shirt Alex said he liked. I didn't think. I simply hit 'add to cart'. He'd get over it when he saw the shirt. He said himself it was the one he liked. I didn't care if he'd be mad. I was doing it for him. He'd deal. And he'd have a cool new shirt at the end of it all. I knew he'd thank me, eventually.

There was nothing to do after I placed the order. I paced around my apartment until I reached the kitchen. I looked over at the sink. There was a coffee mug to the left that I had neglected to wash the night before. How could I have missed that? I turned on the hot water and began to scrub at it. It had a smudge that would just not come off, so I scrubbed harder. Eventually, I got the smudge off, but I felt my temper flare. It was extraordinarily annoying, that smudge. As was the dirt on the side of the counter that I hadn't noticed earlier. I grabbed a clean sponge and began to wipe down all the counters. This turned into a cleaning rampage. I had all the chemicals out. The entire kitchen got scrubbed down. The sink, the counters, the cabinets, the stove, and the floor. Nothing was unclean after I was done with it. The apartment smelled of bleach and pine after I was done. I looked over at the clock. Only about an hour had passed. I had more time to get stuff done. *If Alex came home to a spotless home, maybe he'd feel more reassured that I was alright and not lingering on the thing with my father,* I thought.

I moved to the living room, sweeping and dusting all around, wiping down surfaces. After that, I made my way through the entire apartment before I realized some time had passed since I last looked at the clock. I walked back into the kitchen and saw the time on the digital microwave clock. It was already 2:57 PM. Luna was due to get dropped off any minute now, and I wasn't at the bus stop to greet her.

"Fuck! Fuck! Fuck!" I yelled as I scrambled to get out the door. It took me a minute or two to walk down to the bus stop to wait for Luna normally. Not having that luxury today, I sprinted like a madwoman. I made it down the street exactly as her bus pulled up. I was panting and perspiring, out of breath and physically exhausted from running like that. My heart was nearly thundering out of my chest with effort, feeding into the buzzing that lay just underneath my skin. Sprinting was something I hadn't done since high school.

Luna made her way off the bus and immediately addressed my state.

"Mommy, are you okay? What's wrong?" She asked, her sweet little voice filled with concern.

I was still panting and probably red-faced, but I managed to get out "Mommy's okay... I just... wanted to try... running down here." I disguised my panic from earlier as a fun game.

"Okay, Mommy! Can we run home, too?" She asked. I regretted telling her I wanted to try running.

"Yeah, we can run home, Baby," I got out. I tried to steady my breathing, but failed. "One, two, three, go!" I said, and we both ran, more of a jog on my end, so I could keep pace with her little legs.

As we ran, she shrieked with laughter, enjoying the silly challenge I had unknowingly introduced. I smiled. Her laughter was one of my favorite sounds in the world, and to hear it so uninhibited was an entire experience. I felt bad for people who would never meet Luna. She was such a bright light in the world.

When we got back home, I checked her backpack for any homework she may have had. There was nothing in it. Lucky Luna. I looked around and realized I'd left the cleaning chemicals out. Where Luna could reach them. I scrambled to get them put away before she noticed while she was using the bathroom. How could I have been so careless? I knew Luna had an oral fixation, and if she put her mouth on any of these things... I didn't want to think about it. *Get it together, bitch. You could've poisoned your kid!* I thought harshly.

My stomach growled, and I remembered that I hadn't stopped to eat. *Damn it. Just another thing for Alex to worry over.* It seemed like no matter what I did, nothing would be enough. The strangest thing was that I didn't feel hungry, yet the physical demand for food was there. I decided to ignore it long enough to get things in order.

By the time I'd put away all the cleaning chemicals, Luna had come out of the bathroom. Since she had no homework, she was free to play until dinner time. She knew that. She looked at me, her little face etched with worry.

"What's up, Baby? Are you sad?" I asked, wanting to know what I could do to fix her concern.

"Mommy, the house is different," she pointed out. She must've meant how clean everything was.

"I know, Luna. I cleaned it. Does that bother you?"

"Yeah," she said simply. "I don't like the house different."

I immediately felt a pang of sadness in my chest. I was trying to get the house clean for Alex, but I didn't even consider how it might've made Luna feel. She was very sensitive to changes in her environment. The apartment wasn't particularly messy. I went slightly overboard with cleaning, quite literally everything. Dusting, sweeping, mopping, and cleaning the glass. The works.

"I'm sorry, Sweetheart. I know it's different now, but it'll feel like home again soon, okay?" I told her.

Why did I have to go and clean all that? I knew logically that Luna hated it when her environment was changed a lot. I should've at least left her bedroom alone, but no, that was vacuumed and dusted, too. In addition, I also made her bed and put a fresh wax melt in her room. A scent she was unfamiliar with. I picked 'warm autumn days' and didn't even think it through. Normally,

Luna got to pick her own scents, but hers had faded days ago, and she hadn't picked a new one, so I did. I changed a key element in her room without her knowledge or consent. No wonder she looked upset.

"Mommy, what are you doing?" Luna asked as I walked towards her wax warmer to turn it off.

"I'm gonna let you pick your smell, Lulu. I just gotta clean this one out first."

"But I like that one."

I stopped what I was doing. If she liked the scent, why was she upset? I turned to her and just stared at her.

"I thought you didn't like the house different?" I asked.

"I don't, but that smelled nice," she reiterated.

I put her wax warmer back where it belonged. Noted. She liked 'warm autumn days'.

"Are you hungry, Luna? Do you want me to make you a snack?" I asked, feeling a bit annoyed. I was trying to fix things up for her and Alex, but there she was, confusing me. She didn't like the apartment to be different, but liked the scent in her room. *Make up your mind, kid,* I thought.

"No, I'm not hungry," she replied. "Can I color?"

The annoyance grew. She was upset about the changes one minute and then fine the next. Way to give someone whiplash.

"Yeah, you can color. Mommy needs a moment, and then I'll get your crayons for you," I told her, trying to keep my tone bright and cheerful. I stalked off to the bathroom to take a moment and let myself calm down. Smoking any weed wasn't an option, as Luna was still up, but I wanted to in that moment. I wasn't far from snapping at her for making an innocent remark, and I knew it, so I needed to take my time. I breathed and focused on the cold tile beneath my feet, letting the physical sensation ground me.

Once the feeling had subsided, I stepped out of the bathroom and got Luna her crayons. *What is with me lately?* I wondered.

# 5

# The Price of Impulse

Dinner was going to be pretty simple, as I didn't have time to make anything elaborate since I spent the day cleaning, and was still waiting for my time slot to go pick up the ordered groceries. I went to the kitchen as Luna colored at the dining table, determined to look for something I could whip up quickly. Chicken? No, that needed time to thaw if I wanted to cook with it. I knew we still had some spaghetti noodles. Yeah. Spaghetti was a good, safe option that I knew Luna would actually eat.

    I got the cooking pot from under the lower cabinet, filled it at the sink, put it on the stove, and waited for the water to boil. Luna was singing cheerfully in the living room while I cooked. I leaned my head around the corner of the kitchen to get a look at her. She was coloring away happily, her little pigtails bobbing around as she sang and colored, unaware of my watchful gaze. I couldn't get it out of my head that I left the cleaning chemicals out when she was home. Or that I was so late picking her up from the bus stop. What was that about? Why did I lose track of time like that?

    Just as the water came to a boil, I heard Alex walk in the door. Was it already time for him to be home? I looked at the clock. It was just past 6, so yeah, it was. *Guess I got a late start on dinner, somehow.*

    "Hey, Honey. Dinner is running a little late, but we're having spaghetti tonight," I announced loudly from the kitchen. I had started adding the spaghetti noodles to the pot, refusing to break them like a damned heathen.

"The apartment looks fantastic, Brina. What, did you spend all day on your hands and knees scrubbing?" Alex said as he entered the kitchen, smiling at me warmly.

"Something like that. Sorry about dinner. I lost track of time. Also, I knew we needed groceries, so I set up a pick-up order that should be ready in about half an hour or so. You okay with Luna while I go pick that up?" I asked, trying to show him that I could be productive in the right way.

"Wow. On top of it tonight, huh? No worries about dinner being late. And yeah, I've got Luna. You did awesome today, Hun," he said as he lifted my chin to look at me before planting a kiss on my lips. I smiled in return.

"How was work? Did your boss ever figure out who was stealing from the vending machine?" I inquired, genuinely curious.

"That's a story to share over dinner. The short answer is yes, but it's really freaking funny."

I wondered what could've been so funny about someone stealing. I'm sure it was funny, but I failed to see how.

I got the second pot out from under the cabinet and poured in the sauce, placing it over the unoccupied burner that I'd just turned on. The noodles were about halfway done, so it was perfect timing to heat the sauce and add my spices. I added a bit of powdered garlic and onion for a small kick. Luna had already had this exact meal before, and I knew she liked garlic, so it was perfect.

"Mommy, what are you doing?" I heard Luna ask.

"Making spaghetti. Are you hungry now?" I replied.

"Yes, Mommy. I'm sooo hungry. I'm starving. Spaghetti, please," she whined as her hands flew to her clearly starving little belly. As if she didn't eat lunch at school that day.

I smirked. "Okay, Baby. Dinner is gonna be ready very soon, alright? Why don't you go color some more and give it about another 5 minutes?" I knew it wouldn't be much longer until dinner was ready. She did skip her afternoon snack, so maybe she really did feel like she was starving. I, on the other hand, still had no appetite, but I planned to make myself a small bowl, in case Alex got onto me about eating.

Soon, the noodles were done and strained. I made everybody's bowls, mixing a lot of sauce in my own bowl to hide the lack of noodles. I knew he would make a big deal out of it if he saw I wasn't hungry, so I had to eat something.

"Dinner is ready, you two! Come get your bowls," I commanded. I would make dinner, but fuck trying to carry three bowls out at the same time. I already did my time as a restaurant server, and I was not going to do that again.

Luna and Alex came into the kitchen and got their respective bowls, Luna's being smaller than his and bright pink.

Once we were all seated at the table, I asked Alex to recount his funny vending machine story.

"Okay, so you remember that one guy? Davey? Not even cool Dave. Fuuu-reaking Davey," Alex said, quickly correcting his near profane slip in front of Luna. "Anyway, the guy figured out that if he just mashed the asterisk button a bunch of times, it would eventually spit out random candy bars. But the thing is, you have to do it rapidly, like a fast-paced fighter game. So there he was spamming away at the machine, and boss man comes out from behind him and asks what he thought he was doing. The guy panicked and told him the truth. Showed him how to do it and gave him a candy bar. He got a write-up, but now we all know how to get free candy bars. Unless they replace the machine, which I doubt they will if we play it smart."

I heard a ping from my phone, but I didn't move to check it immediately. I was too focused on eating the small amount of spaghetti I had given myself and listening to Alex's explanation of the work debacle. It was most likely the grocery order that was ready for pickup.

"Was that your phone, Honey? Is it important?" Alex asked, his mouth half full of spaghetti.

"Close your mouth when you're eating. You're setting a bad example," I pointed out to him, gesturing to Luna next to us. He quickly stopped talking, only pausing to roll his eyes at me. I smirked. "And it was most likely the grocery order I placed. I'll go pick it up after dinner if you're all good with Luna."

Alex swallowed the food in his mouth. "Sounds like a solid plan to me. Luna and I will be just fine at home for the 20 minutes it takes to pick up groceries."

*20 minutes, huh? I bet I could cut that time in half if I moved quickly enough,* I thought. I finished the last bits of my spaghetti and rose from the table to put my bowl in the sink. Once I'd rinsed it out, I left the kitchen, entered the living room, and grabbed my purse off the coffee table before heading for the front door.

"I'll be back. Luna, be good for your father, okay? If you are, you can have dessert when I get back. Daddy will tell me if you're good or not."

"Okay, Mommy! Donuts?" She requested.

I smiled because I ordered donuts in the grocery pickup, knowing how much she loved them. "I think that can be arranged. Mommy loves you both," I said as I left the apartment, not needing the reply, knowing they both loved me.

I got in my car and sped towards the grocery store, ignoring the speed limit. Testing the limits of my speed was a fun challenge I was ready to accept. I wanted to see exactly how fast I could get there and back. I wanted to surprise Alex with the quick trip and a new shirt. Once he saw it, I knew he'd love it. So what if I spent a little extra to get it? I simply wanted Alex to have something I knew he wanted.

I arrived in the designated pickup spot at the grocery store and pushed the button on my phone to indicate that I'd arrived. I sat and waited for the worker to come out and load up my car. He was surprisingly quick. Got everything in the trunk in under a minute. Color me impressed. He told me to have a good day, and I sped off again.

I raced through stop lights and barely stopped at stop signs, choosing to slightly slow down before I blasted through them. Speeding came naturally to me. As I approached the street my home was on, I decided to test how well the brakes worked and sped nearly to my parking spot before screeching the car to a stop, luckily not leaving any tire tracks on the street.

It didn't take me long at all to get home. I looked at the clock in the car. I was gone for 14 minutes. Less than the 20 Alex estimated. It was pretty lucky that we lived so close to the store. I got out of the car and started grabbing groceries. There weren't a lot of bags, but I knew a few of them were heavy. Did I want to risk carrying them all at once? Absolutely. More than one trip out for the groceries was for whiners and quitters. I hooked all the bags between my two arms and made a beeline for the apartment door, moving quickly so I didn't lose my strength.

I opened the door and walked in to a very excitable Luna.

"Donuts!" She hollered, demanding them.

"Say 'please', Luna," Alex directed to her.

"Please!" She added, her little hand outstretched towards me.

"Alex, help me get these put away. Afterwards, we'll get you some donuts, Luna," I said as I moved towards the kitchen, groceries weighing down on me.

I placed them all on the floor in their bags and got to work putting them all away. I started with the cold items first, and Alex soon joined me in the kitchen, helping me with the cold food.

"What the? Did they give you part of someone else's or…der?" His voice stalled when his hands found black fabric. He pulled out the shirt. This was it. The moment I'd anticipated.

"I know you wanted me to wait to get it, but I saw how much you liked this shirt, so I went ahead and got it for you! What do you think?" I beamed, certain Alex would love his surprise. I waited and watched for his reaction. It wasn't what I'd expected.

His grip on the T-shirt tightened so much his knuckles started to turn white. I saw his jaw clench. His eyes lacked their usual jovial look, replaced by what I knew to be anger.

"Luna, come get your donuts and take them to your room. Mommy and Daddy need to have a very important talk," he said, every word short and clipped.

"Okay, Daddy!" She exclaimed happily, oblivious to the sudden shift in Alex's demeanor. He handed her the package of donuts, and she ran off to her room, giggling like a little goblin that was about to devour all of them. I watched as she shut her door, her smile unwavering and huge. She normally wasn't allowed to eat in her room, but I guessed Alex had made this exception.

He leaned back against the counter, his hands gripping the edge. He took a deep breath and looked at me. "So, you lied to me." He started. I was surprised. I genuinely thought he'd liked the shirt.

"Alex," I pleaded.

"You lied to me and went behind my back to buy that fucking shirt. What the actual hell, Sabrina?! What? Was that whole cleaning spree something to butter me up? To make up for the fact that you went against me?" He questioned harshly.

The light ecstatic feeling I had previously dissipated. Alex's words hit me like cold water hit a hot stove. *How dare he yell at me for this?*

"I don't even know why you're mad! The damn shirt is for you! It's not like I just dropped a grand on clothes for myself or something. And no, I cleaned the apartment because it needed to be done and I had the energy to do it," I retorted with exasperation, gesturing towards Alex with my arm.

He paused. Something clicked in his head, and I could see the gears turning in his head.

"What?" I asked, dropping my arms to my sides.

"Be honest with me right now. Are you manic? Don't even think about lying to me."

That did it. The lid was off. It had boiled over. There was no lid anymore. I was beyond livid. I could feel my face and body heat with fury.

"What the hell, Alex?! I've had a few difficult days, and suddenly I'm manic?! Am I allowed to do anything without being accused of being in an episode? Seriously? What an asshole-ish thing to say!"

"Well, maybe if you weren't acting like it, I wouldn't have said anything!"

"No, you know what? Screw you. I busted my ass to get this place clean for our family, and I bought you that shirt and fucking sweet treats because I knew you'd like them. All for this to get turned around on me. I'm not hypomanic, which is the term for bipolar 2, by the way. You'd know that if you'd bothered to do the research on my diagnosis!" I yelled, my voice cracking at the end.

"Don't even start, Brina. You know I did my research. I got confused about one term, okay? That isn't the issue here. You realize if you're manic, or hypomanic, we should get you help, right?" Alex said. I didn't need help. I was fine.

"I'm. Not. Fucking. Manic!" I enunciated each syllable through gritted teeth.

"Okay! Damn! You're not manic! I'll stop asking. But why the shirt, Brina? We talked about it. You agreed to wait until after Luna's party. What happened to the plan we set?"

I sighed for a long moment and rubbed my temples with my fingers. The buzzing feeling under my skin felt less like a vibration and more like an angry swarm of bees trying to burst from within me. Why did everything have to be planned? Why couldn't I be spontaneous? Especially over something so small. I closed my eyes and leaned back against a wall.

"I don't know. I saw an ad for it, so I added it to the cart when I was getting ready to check out. I really thought you'd like it," I explained.

Alex's gaze softened, and his grip on the counter loosened.

"I wish you hadn't bought it when you did, but I need you to take it back. You can return it tomorrow and get the store credit for it. Sabrina, we can't have any more of this. Please. I can't take any more impulse spending. We need to save money for a few more weeks, long enough to get the money saved up for Luna's birthday presents. I mean it. No more."

We rarely ever fought, but it felt like that's all we were doing lately. Today was going pretty well until this fight, too. I got so much done. I really felt accomplished. And then he had to go and get all defensive over saving money once again. I thought we had plenty to get Luna exactly what she wanted, but Alex disagreed. He wanted to get her something bigger, and I agreed at the time. I regretted it then.

# 6

# Driven Up a Wall

Two weeks had flown by since my fight with Alex. I felt awful for upsetting him, and I returned the shirt like he had told me to. I wished he hadn't assumed I was manic just because I wanted a bit of spontaneity. As much as I wanted to back off from the D&D campaign I was creating, I couldn't resist the call, but I still made sure to get regular daily chores taken care of. Alex didn't understand how much free time I had during the week, so it was only natural that I gravitated towards the campaign.

Hell, he should've been happy I wasn't going shopping instead, as I really wanted to. I had the idea to make myself a fantasy outfit suited for a dungeon master who gets really into their campaign. I wanted to make Alex an outfit for the campaign as well, but he hadn't spoken about what kind of character he'd want to play as yet. My plan was to go buy all the fabric I wanted for the outfits, along with all the accessories I wanted to include. It would have been a lot. Probably more money than we actually had, but you couldn't put a price on creativity.

My appetite was nearly absent, but I managed to make myself eat at least once a day. Well, at least every other day. I was too wrapped up in writing the backstory and important scenes that could potentially happen to guide Alex's character along. I still drank a lot of soda and went out a few times a week to my favorite coffee shop to work on the campaign in a different location, so some calories were making their way into my system. That was better than nothing, I supposed. I didn't question it.

The meal I ate was always dinner with Luna and Alex, so that they could see me eating. Alex got worried on nights when I said I didn't feel hungry, so I started forcing myself to eat dinner with him and our daughter. I wanted them to see I was fine and in control. I knew something was off, but I couldn't place it. It felt like I no longer needed food or as much sleep as other people because I was functioning fine without them. At least, that's what I thought.

I'd recently stepped on the scale and saw I was down by more than a few pounds—at least 5 within the last week. I kept to my regular schedule of weighing myself once a week. The week before, I was about 155 pounds. I was now around 150. *That wasn't too bad. I'd been meaning to drop those pounds anyway,* I thought. If anybody else had dropped the weight like I had, I probably would've said it wasn't healthy. But this wasn't someone else. This was me. I was different. I could keep it under control.

Luna had a parent-teacher conference coming up that evening, and I was determined to be there for it. I wanted her teacher to see me as a super-involved parent, because that's what I was. I brought snacks for the class, volunteered at every school function, and made appreciation cards for all the staff who I knew regularly interacted with Luna. I was really on top of things.

"You ready to go, Alex?" I asked as I grabbed my purse off the coffee table. I wanted to make an impression, so I dressed in business casual attire; however, the maroon dress I chose hugged my figure tightly. It was long enough to cover my thighs but ended at my knees. Was it too much? Possibly. Alex's attire was a simple T-shirt and jeans.

"Just about. I've just gotta get the keys and we can go. Was Luna alright when you dropped her off with my mom?" He said, searching the pristine living room for his missing keys. I took his car earlier, so there was a good chance his keys were still in my purse. I dug around and sure enough, there they were.

"I've got your keys. And Luna was fine. She was so thrilled to see her grandma that she forgot all about me and ran straight to her. Little booger." An idea came to me. "Would you mind if I drove tonight?" Alex was normally the one who drove when the two of us were going to the same destination. He raised an eyebrow at me, and I met him with a smile as sweet as the treats he craved.

"I mean, if you want to, go for it. What's gotten into you?" He questioned with a smile on his face.

"I feel like driving. Don't you ever get like that? I was also thinking, since your mom has Luna for the night, why don't we have a date after the conference? Just go somewhere we haven't been before. Eat something new. Something different from what we're used to. I really don't feel like cooking tonight," I got out quickly. I was thrilled at the idea of spending time with Alex outside of our home. Since he started wanting us to save money, we hadn't had a single date night. I was determined to change that then and there. Plus, if it had to do with food, he was more likely to say yes.

Alex frowned slightly, then regained his smile, somewhat brighter than it had been before.

"You know what? Fuck it. One night won't break the bank. Let's just keep our meal under fifty dollars. Fair?" He agreed.

I literally bounced up and down with glee. A smile that nearly ripped my face apart was abundantly clear on my face.

"More than fair! Thank you, Honey! Do you wanna pick where we go, or would you like me to? I've kinda been wanting to try that new Thai place that just opened up in the next town over," I suggested.

"Yeah, that sounds alright to me. I heard they have massive portions for a relatively modest price. Apparently, the owner is all about authenticity and imports his ingredients."

I cocked my head to the side. "Where did you hear that? Coworker?" I asked, curious. Alex normally didn't have that much information about places we wanted to go. He generally had a relaxed attitude toward our meals when we ate out.

"Yeah. You remember Davey, the vending machine thief from work? Turns out his cousin works there as a waiter. They're fairly close, so I got a lot of details from Davey since he was busy running his mouth instead of doing his job. Wouldn't it be great if he put the same amount of effort into his job as he does into talking to others? Maybe then working with him would be worth it,"

Alex chuckled. I missed whatever was funny, my mind running a million miles a minute and unable to fully pay attention to him, but laughed anyway, not wanting him to feel disappointed that his attempt at humor was lost to me.

I pulled the car keys from my purse and made my way to the front door, ready to leave for the parent-teacher conference. Alex followed behind me, probably taking the chance to stare at his favorite asset of mine. I didn't mind, so I acted oblivious.

I reached the driver's side door and unlocked it manually since the key fob was still not working. I really hoped he would get it fixed soon. I knew it was only seconds, but it would save us a bit of time getting in the car. I made a mental note to get the key fob fixed soon if Alex wouldn't.

He sat in the passenger seat, adjusting it so he could have more legroom. I normally sat in that spot, so when he got in, he nearly banged his knees on the dashboard. I laughed at how silly he looked trying to sit comfortably at first. He shot me a quick, stern look, and I stifled my laughter, a smile still playing at my lips.

I started the car once all the mirrors were adjusted, quickly putting on my seat belt as did Alex. Once his was on, I quickly shifted from park to drive and took off from the normal parking spot, a wide grin on my face.

"Easy there, Hun," Alex said as his hand flew to what we lovingly called the 'oh shit' handle at the side of the car's roof. His eyes were wide with panic. I didn't react. I just kept driving, sped up, and giggled.

"You'll be fine. Don't worry. I got my license before you, remember? I've got experience on my side. We're fine," I assured him.

"Brina, I'm serious. Slow down. You're scaring me," he stated. I laughed at him again. Looking at the speedometer, I saw that I was only going maybe 15 or so miles over the speed limit. I'd done this before on the interstate, so I wasn't scared. I had a good grasp on how to drive fast. Alex needed to chill and let me drive.

"We're fine, my love. I've got this," I said quickly. Something inside me felt like I needed to go fast, and I was going to indulge it. It wouldn't be the first time I've sped. The world around me hurried by in a beautiful barrage of fallen autumn leaves. Shades of red, orange, yellow, and brown all colored the roads and sidewalks as I drove by. I loved every shade.

"You're gonna get us a speeding ticket if you don't slow down. And there's a curve coming up. Please slow down, Brina," he pleaded.

I ignored him and even sped up, the turn causing both of us to shift in our seats in the direction of the curve, but I still had control of the car. I felt on top of the world, giggling at the sensation. That was a phenomenal feeling. I'd never felt so alive.

"Pull over now!" Alex bellowed, his face red with anger.

The sudden outburst caused me to jump and swerve.

"Sabrina!" He exclaimed. I had jumped a curb.

I found a gas station to pull over at and parked the car in a vacant space. I was furious that he had called me by my full first name. He knew I hated it. I used to get compared to a certain teenage witch with the same name. Kids were mean.

"What the hell, Alex? We were fine until you yelled at me!" I demanded.

"You hopped a fucking curb!" He yelled pointedly.

"Yeah, after you yelled at me! And don't call me that! You know how much I hate it."

"What the hell were you thinking?! Why were you speeding like that? You could've gotten us pulled over. Or worse, hurt or killed! And give me my keys back, right now. We're switching seats. I'm driving from now on. Forget about date night. I'm too pissed at you." He opened his door and got out, motioning for me to do the same.

I huffed and reluctantly opened my door, getting out as slowly as possible just to annoy him. What was his deal? I was fine until he started yelling at me. I had control of the car, no cops had stopped us, and the road was practically empty. I wasn't going to hurt anyone, especially not us. I was angry about the date night thing, but after thinking it through, I wondered why I would have wanted to go out with someone who didn't trust my judgment that night. *He's being a prick,* I thought as I deliberately walked past him, not meeting his gaze.

I reached the passenger side door and hesitated, my hand hovering just above the handle. Alex was already in the car and waiting for me to get in. *Why should I give him what he wants?*

I stepped back from the car and walked towards the entry to the gas station. I didn't realize it was the one not far from our apartment. The same cashier from that day I was so angry was in the corner, and I guessed he recognized me because his posture instantly shifted when I walked in. I walked over to the refrigerated sodas and got myself one. *Only one. Fuck Alex,* I thought. As I went to pay, my red-faced husband appeared in the store. I ignored him, but he made it very difficult. He walked right up to me and tried to force eye contact, but I stared ahead, making eye contact with the increasingly anxious cashier.

I finished my transaction and spun on my heel with my drink in hand. I tried to open the passenger side door, only to find it locked. *Fucking Alex. Of course, he'd lock me out. He's really pissed.* I groaned. He was going to make me talk about what was going through my head and call me reckless. I didn't want to hear it.

Alex appeared from inside the store quickly and walked over to the car, crossing his arms and looking at me expectantly.

"Well?" He asked.

"Don't 'well' me. I said what I had to say. We were fine, and you panicked for no reason. If you hadn't yelled at me, I never would've bounced off the curb. That was all you," I spat out.

"Oh, so going nearly twenty miles over the speed limit is normal for you? You have that kind of experience. Hmm, I wonder how often you do that with Luna in the car. Should I ask her?" He asked me sardonically. I saw red.

"I'd never speed with Luna in the car! You fucking know that! I'd never, ever put her at risk! Have you lost your mind?!" I demanded, getting in his face, poking my finger into his chest as I yelled.

He took a step back and held up his hands, showing he wasn't going to push further. His face blanched as I took another step towards him, refusing to back down.

"Is everything okay here, sir?" I heard a man's voice call out. I looked in the direction of the voice, fury still clear on my face, but it quickly faded as I saw a police car and a uniformed officer poking his head out in the spot next to Alex's car.

Alex gave me a look that told me to keep quiet. I didn't want to comply with anything he told me to do right then, but I knew I absolutely needed to, so I didn't get arrested.

"We're fine. Just a disagreement," Alex told the officer. He didn't look convinced, but pulled his head back into his car. I let out a breath I didn't realize I was holding. I was still angry with Alex for insinuating that I would ever speed with Luna in the car. That was something I did either alone or with my friends. They never saw a problem with it. They thought it was fun, even. But not Alex. He'd always been a stickler for traffic laws. It was one thing we disagreed on. I often went with the general saying that five is fine, ten is a fine when it came to my speeding. I knew that and still decided to drive extra fast with him in the car. What had gotten into me?

The officer had gotten out of his car and walked right up to Alex, who still looked a bit pale and nervous.

"Are you sure it was just a disagreement, sir? Because from what I saw-"

"He said we're fine. Don't you listen?" I popped off out of nowhere, not liking this pig prying further into what was supposed to be between my husband and me.

"Ma'am, back up and watch your tone with me. I asked him. Not you. You'll have your chance to speak when we're done."

I started to take a step towards the officer, ready to give him a piece of my mind, but Alex put his arm in front of me, shaking his head.

"It's fine, Officer. We're good. Thank you for checking on us." Alex started leading me towards the passenger side door, which was still locked. He tried to click it open with his key fob, but he forgot that the battery was dead in the fob itself.

"Stay right here. Don't move." He directed me as if he were scolding a child. I crossed my arms, shifting my weight to one side, but I did as he said.

The officer had walked inside after a final glance our way, seemingly convinced our situation was under control. Alex manually unlocked the door on his side of the car and pointed to the passenger side seat, silently demanding I get in. I rolled my eyes and did as I was told, with as much contempt as I could manage. I made unwavering eye contact with him as he got in the car.

He broke it and looked at the clock on the dashboard.

"Fuck. We're gonna be late to Luna's parent-teacher conference. We were supposed to be there 3 minutes ago." He ran his hand through his long hair and let out a sigh. He looked over at me with a scowl on his face. "This is benched for now. We need to get it together long enough to talk to her teacher. Got it?" He said to me, leaving no room for argument.

I mumbled something about getting there early if he wouldn't have stopped me from driving, but ultimately said, "Fine. Let's hurry up and get this over with." My arms stayed crossed as he pulled out of the gas station.

The drive to the school was silent. When we got there, her teacher was waiting for us at the door of her classroom. A woman with dyed burgundy hair and smart reading glasses. I remembered her name was Ms. Reign from meet-the-teacher night. She looked annoyed. Probably because we made her wait as long as we did.

"You're Luna's parents. Please, take a seat." She gestured to the chairs in front of her desk, giving us a quick, forced smile.

Alex and I sat in our respective chairs, the tension between us palpable.

"So, Luna is doing extremely well with help from her BCBA. She's little Miss Popular. Everyone knows who she is. Her handwriting has come a long way, as has her speech. Overall, she's an absolute joy to have in class. Always quick to help her peers if they're struggling."

That last sentence made me focus on the task at hand. Luna was helping others? Why hadn't I seen that before? My heart swelled with pride, and a genuine smile formed on my face. My girl was a helper. I was worried about her capabilities as she got older, whether she'd struggle to make friends or have people understand her, but those fears had been dashed by what her teacher had said.

"I'm so incredibly happy to hear that! Is there anything we can do to help her build from here?" I asked brightly.

Ms. Reign gave me another smile, this one less forced.
"From what I can tell, you're already doing everything you can to ensure she grows up to be a wonderful person. You show up for her school functions, make sure her homework is done every night, and she almost always comes in with a smile and a story about how you and her father played with her. You're

probably some of the most hands-on parents we have." She chuckled a bit, and I smiled at her. Alex had a stoic look on his face, but managed a small smile for Ms. Reign.

"Alright, so unless you have any questions, I'd say we're good to wrap up. Anything you'd like to know?" She asked, pausing for us to reply.

"No, I think we're good. You were pretty concise, ma'am," Alex stated respectfully.

She rose from her chair, and so did we. She walked us out of the classroom, and I saw another couple waiting at the door. They were probably her next appointment.

Alex and I walked out of the school and made it all the way back to the car before he spoke to me.

"What were you thinking? What exactly was going through your head?" Alex asked me.

For a moment, I'd forgotten about our most recent fight. I sighed exasperatedly and leaned against the passenger side door.

"I don't know, Alex. I wanted to go fast. It's fine. I've done it dozens of times, and I know where the cops hide out with radar guns. They wouldn't have caught me."

"And if there was a drunk driver on the road, swerving all over the place, I'm sure you'd be fine then, right?" He gestured to me with a free hand as he unlocked the car.

He had a point there, but I wasn't going to let him know that.

"Yeah, I would. I'd pull over and get out of his way. Then, I'd call the cops. Like any sane, rational person would," I stated as I got in the car.

"Brina. Stop. Just stop. For the love of everything, can you just admit when you're in the wrong and stop trying to justify it? You put us in danger, and for what? Fun? An adrenaline rush?" His eyes bore into mine, searching for an answer I didn't have.

I broke the intense eye contact and fidgeted with my hands, interlocking my fingers together and twisting them.

"I don't know. I wanted that feeling of going fast, and I was fine until you yelled at me. Seriously, you cannot yell at me when I'm driving. If anything puts us in danger, it's that," I pointed out.

Alex ran a hand over his face and groaned.

"Of course. Of course, you're gonna keep justifying. Why kid myself? Brina, I can't keep doing this. Please. Please promise me you won't speed like that anymore. I refuse to lose you because you want some temporary high. We aren't moving until you promise you won't speed," he stated. He took the keys out of the ignition and placed them in his rear pocket.

He was trying to back me into a corner. Trying to force me to comply with him. I wasn't having it. I grabbed the handle and opened my door.

"What are you doing? Brina." He asked, panic rising in his voice.

"You can't control me, Alex," I said as I got out of the car, pulling my phone from my purse.

"Brina, get back in the car."

"Go home. I'll get there my own way. At my own pace. If I do it fast, so be it." I spat as I walked away from the car back towards the school. I looked through my contacts and found exactly who I wanted to call. Scarlet. She was one of the few friends I'd made since moving up to be closer to Alex's family. She started as my hairstylist, but that quickly turned into coffee dates and hanging out at each other's places. Alex and Scarlet got along well enough, which was a huge plus to me, but in that moment? I didn't give a flying fuck what he thought.

I dialed the number, and she picked up after a few rings.

"Hello?" I heard her ask.

"Hey, Scar. Do you think you could come grab me? Alex and I had a bit of a blowout. Wanna grab a drink or two? I'll give you all the details."

"Sure. I've got nothing going on right now. Where are you? I'll be right there."

I watched as Alex pulled away from the parking lot. He was actually leaving me there. *Asshole.* I gave Scarlet the address for the school and sat on the curb to wait for her.

# 7

# Adios

I continued to sit on that curb for about half an hour, my thoughts running cyclically. *Why did he have to push me? Why couldn't he just let me drive? We were fine. Absolutely fine. Alex is being a difficult ass. He needs to chill the hell out and simply trust that I knew what I was doing.* I didn't know what had gotten into him. All I knew was that I was starting to get fed up waiting for Scarlet to show. I knew she lived a little further away from the school than I did, but damn. She was taking her sweet time coming to get me.

Just as I was about to call her again to find out how far she was, my friend's silver car rolled up. She honked twice at me, making me jump, as she rolled down her window. I could make out her distinctive curly purple hair. She had her makeup done up as well, looking like some beauty guru.

"Damn, Brina. You look hot as hell. Get it, bitch!" She exclaimed as she got a good look at my outfit. I got up from the curb, and I could hear her let out a low whistle as I opened the passenger side door.

"Were you planning on going out? It looks like you were gonna hit up a club or something," she remarked as I sat down and shut the car door. I looked over her outfit, seeing that she was wearing a revealing V-neck dress herself.

"I mean, Alex and I were supposed to have a date night after the parent-teacher conference, but nope. He had to go and be a controlling asshole." I threw my arms into the air with frustration. Scarlet motioned for me to put my seat belt on as she started to pull away from the school's parking lot. I complied and asked her if I could put on some music.

"Nuh-uh. My car, my tunes. You know the rules," she stated, giving me a mischievous grin. I pouted at her, but ultimately accepted her answer. "So, what was your fight about?" She asked as she continued driving, eyes shifting between me and the road, brows raised.

"Girl, he was just being a big baby. I sped a little on the way to the parent-teacher conference. Big whoop. You've been in the car with me speeding before. Have you ever felt like you were in danger?" I asked, trying to prove a point.

"I mean, no, but I get where he's coming from. Not everybody is okay with speeding, B," she stated as she continued driving. I swung my head in her direction and glared at her.

"I thought you were supposed to be on my side. You're my friend," I spat out, angry that she was defending my husband. Scarlet rolled her eyes at me, not phased by my shitty mood.

"Chill, girl. I'm on your side. I'm just saying that not everybody is okay with the way you drive. Let's change the subject. What drink do you think you're gonna want to start with when we get to the bar? I'm thinking a Sex on the Beach for myself."

I thought about it for a moment. I didn't want a single drink. I wanted shots. Something I could slam back fast and get a buzz going quickly. I knew I could convince Scarlet to do at least one or two with me.

"I'm thinking I want an adios shot. Say goodbye to this shitty ass day, you know?" I looked at my friend and raised a single eyebrow at her, silently issuing a challenge.

"I don't know what that is, but it sounds great. What's in it?"

"Vodka, gin, rum, tequila, that blue stuff they add to fruity drinks that tastes like oranges. A few mixers. It's strong as fuck," I rattled off to her, counting the ingredients off on my fingers and smiling brightly.

"Shit. That sounds insane. I'll have one, but I don't think I can do more than that if I'm driving."

I rolled my eyes at her and laughed. "You gotta learn to live life on the edge. Couldn't you ask your boyfriend to come get us after? Let loose. I swear, you've become so domestic since you two have gotten together. It's a little sickening."

She let out a small, exaggerated gasp, then joined me in my laughter, knowing I didn't mean anything by it. Hell, since she'd been with Tom, she'd learned so many recipes to make for him that it'd become a hobby. She held monthly dinners for me and a few of her other friends, where she'd just make a full spread of what she'd learned in the last few weeks or so. I loved those dinners and always stayed after to help her wash dishes. But I figured she needed a break from all that for one night. Tom could fend for himself.

We'd finally made it to the parking lot of the bar. I quickly got out, and my purse fell behind me and whacked me in the back, but I didn't care. I was excited to let loose with a good friend. Hurrying over to Scarlet's door before she could get to the handle, I opened it for her.

"Milady, allow me," I joked, bowing my head and offering my hand to her.

"Thank you, madam," she giggled, and accepted my outstretched hand, curtsying. "God, we're weird."

"It's the only way to live. Fuck what other people think. Now come on, bitch! Let's have some fun!" I exclaimed, practically dragging her into the bar by her hand.

As we entered the bar, the first thing I noticed was that Scarlet and I were overdressed. There were a couple of burly-looking guys sitting in the back corner of the bar, who had nudged each other when they saw Scarlet and me enter. They were both dressed in casual jeans and T-shirts. The bartender was a brunette woman who immediately nodded her head to us in greeting, wearing a tight, low-cut black tank top. She was preoccupied washing a shaker. I quickly made my way up to the bar and took a seat, waiting impatiently for her to get to us and take our drink orders. I tapped my foot on the barstool I was sitting on as Scarlet joined me on the stool to my left.

She nudged me as she took her seat. "Stop tapping your foot. That's not going to get her here any faster," she said.

I stopped tapping and rolled my eyes at her. I wasn't hurting anyone, but if it bothered Scarlet, I'd stop. She was one of the few friends I had, and I didn't want to annoy her, no matter how much energy I had to expend.

The bartender rinsed out her shaker and put it down on the drying mat next to the sink before walking up to my friend and me.

"Hey, ladies. What can I get for you?" She asked. I shared a look with Scarlet, and she nodded, smiling.

"Can we get four adios shots?" I asked.

Scarlet swung her head around to me, brows raised and eyes full of shock.

"Four?" She mouthed to me.

"Shh." I shoved her lightly and looked back at the bartender, who had begun pulling different liquors from the shelf behind her and roughly measured each one as she poured the liquids into the newly clean shaker.

"Brina, I'm not doing 2," Scarlet said in a hushed tone.

"Fine, don't. I'll have your other one, then." I grinned widely at her.

"You're trying to get fucked up, aren't you?" She asked, her tone a mix of amusement and concern.

"Abso-fucking-lutely," I replied, completely serious. "I'm going to wipe this day from my memory."

"What about Luna? Don't you have to get back to her tonight?"

"Nope. My mother-in-law has her for the night."

"What about Alex? Won't he be pissed if you come home wasted?"

I rolled my eyes at her once again, frowning a bit.

"I don't care what Alex thinks. It's my liver I'm destroying, not his. He can keep his opinions to himself for once," I said.

The bartender pulled four shot glasses out and poured the blue liquid from the shaker after stirring in some Sprite. I watched as the tiny drinks fizzed slightly and the smile returned to my face. I reached for my purse, pulled out my wallet, and handed my card to her.

"Let's keep an open tab," I instructed.

"You got it!" The bartender replied cheerfully.

"Girl, am I gonna have to carry you out of here tonight? You'd better not barf on me," Scarlet said as she grabbed a shot glass from the counter. I mirrored her action and grabbed my own shot glass. We clinked our glasses, tapped them on the counter, and slammed them back quickly. The shot was incredibly strong with a slightly orange aftertaste. Her face contorted in disgust, and she shook her head.

"That's a lot," she said, coughing a bit.

I laughed at her reaction and reached for another shot. She gave me a look, but I slammed it back anyway. I grabbed the third one before she could take it away from me and poured it down my throat, giggling like a three-year-old who had just gotten caught sneaking a cookie from the jar.

"Whoa, Brina. Take it easy. I promise, you can have more shots, but damn. No need to go ham from the start."  Scarlet looked at me with her brow furrowed in concern.

"Oh, don't you lecture me. I'm fine." I waved my hand in her direction, my head already starting to swim a bit. My gut began to feel warm and fuzzy, heating me up from the inside out. Exactly the feeling I was going for. I didn't need Alex's judgment or hers. "Want me to prove I'm alright?"

"Not really. Look, I'm not one to say no to a good time, but let's not end up praying to the porcelain goddess within the first 3 minutes of being here," she stated, looking back to the four empty shot glasses that were full moments ago.

She had a point. I wasn't planning on going back home anytime soon. I could take my time. Like a fucking lady.

I felt my purse vibrate, pulled my phone out, and groaned. Alex was texting me.

'Where are you?'

I grimaced at my phone.

'Not with you, that's for sure.'

I typed out the last letter quickly and hit send.

I stuffed my phone back in my purse before I felt it buzz again. I considered not checking it, but my curiosity got the better of me as I pulled my phone back out. I could at least read his message. Even if I was just planning to leave him on read.

'Not funny. I'm worried. I can come get you. Tell me where you're at.'

I began to reply, but Scarlet swiped my phone and started messing around on it, grinning the whole time.

"Hey! Give that back," I cried, making a feeble attempt to get my phone as she held it away from my reach.

"You'll get it back after I'm done," she retorted, typing something into it as she spoke.

I made another swipe for it, but the alcohol had made my aim less than stellar. I missed and whacked my arm on the counter with an audible thud.

"Mother-! Mmmm, that hurt," I groaned, holding my injured arm with my good one. That was going to leave a mark.

Scarlet looked me over, laughed, and handed me back my phone. I quickly unlocked it and checked my message thread between my husband and me.

'Don't worry. She's safe. It's Scarlet. I've got her. I'll bring her home later.'

"You could've just, I don't know, asked me for my phone instead of stealing it," I stated, crossing my arms in false annoyance. I quickly put my phone back into my purse and looked over at the bartender, hoping to get some more drinks. At least a water or soda, so Scarlet wouldn't pester me about drinking too much too fast. The bartender was making what I assumed were Jack and Cokes for the two men down at the other end of the bar. They were talking among themselves and stealing glances at Scarlet and me. The two men nodded, grabbed their drinks from the bartender, and stood from their seats, drinks in hand.

"Not this shit," Scarlet said as she shielded her face with her hand, not wanting to be noticed. The men got closer, but stopped a few stools away, allowing their gaze to fall on us as they made not-so-quiet critiques about our appearances. I saw one check out Scarlet's cleavage, and I grabbed her arm to turn her to face me, giving the man a pointed look.

He smirked. I thought he took that as a challenge, and I could feel the once pleasant heat threaten to overwhelm me from my core that had nothing to do with the drinks in my system. Did he really want to try me? Because I was so not in the mood to deal with some drunk assholes.

I tried to ignore them and returned my eyes to my friend's face, which looked incredibly uncomfortable. The bartender approached us once again, seemingly annoyed with the men she had been serving moments ago.

"Can I get you ladies anything else? Water? Sodas? More drinks?" She offered.

"I'll get two more adios shots," I stated with a scowl in the men's direction.

Scarlet looked at me with pure concern on her face. She didn't know what I had planned.

The bartender nodded and made the shots for me, placing them before me with a curious look. I grabbed both shots and whistled at the men. They turned their heads to gape at me, looks of bewilderment plastered on their faces.

"Adios," I started as I took the first shot, "Motherfuckers," I said as I took the second and pointed towards the door.

I watched their faces turn red with indignation, sputtering out incoherent protests. The bartender became tight-lipped and turned her back to us, but I could've sworn I saw her shoulders shaking up and down in silent laughter. I guffawed at their confusion and looked back at my friend.

She was stifling her amusement with her hands over her mouth, snorting after a few seconds. That got me laughing even harder, and I made eye contact with the men once more.

They rose and walked quickly to the exit. As they passed us, I swore I heard one of them say something about us being 'fucking bitches' and I followed through with the impulse I had.

"It's because of dickwads like you!" I yelled, laughing as they hurriedly stormed out the door. The bartender turned to face us once again, holding two bright red drinks in her hands and offering them to us.

"We didn't order these," Scarlet pointed out.

"They're on the house. Those assholes have been in here all day, annoying away my other customers," she stated as she began to clean the shaker beneath the counter.

"Thanks!" I exclaimed as I began to chug the drink.

"Whoa, Brina! That's like six drinks in less than 15 minutes. Slow down," Scarlet scolded me.

*Why the hell was everyone telling me to slow down? Why couldn't they speed up? Get on my level*, I thought. I frowned as I downed the rest of my drink.

"Can you get us two waters, please?" Scarlet asked the bartender. She nodded and got two large cups from the counter below her, filling them with her soda gun. She placed the drinks before us and walked away, giving us some space. I hated that Scarlet was trying to limit me. Just like Alex had tried to.

I shifted in my seat and felt the world tilt on its axis. The world looked fuzzy at the edges of my vision, and the feeling consumed my entire being. It wasn't entirely unpleasant. I could feel it growing and spreading through my entire body. My mood was instantly lifted.

Scarlet side-eyed me as she watched me start to sway slightly in my seat. She took a sip of her water and motioned for me to do the same. I had a smirk on my face as I grabbed my water and started to sip it, making eye contact with her, giggling slightly to myself. I was thinking about the way the two men stormed away, all because they couldn't handle getting called out. I thought it was hilarious.

"What are you giggling about?" Scarlet asked me with a sly smile.

I beamed at her. "I'm not teeellling," I teased in a singsong manner, my inhibitions lowered.

"Oh, you're gone gone. Your face is red. How are you feeling?" She asked further.

"I. Feel. Fantastic," I whispered to her in a broken staccato, trying very hard to remain coherent. I rested my head on her shoulder. I giggled even more, somewhat louder.

"Okay, that's it. You're cut off. Excuse me, Bartender, can you close her tab?" She asked.

I felt a rush of anger wash over me.

"Don't you daaaare -*hic*- cut me off! Tha's rude." I slurred, protesting her order, pointing at my friend accusingly. The bartender was doing something at her register, probably running my card and closing out my tab. I felt my stomach growl at me. I hadn't eaten that day, since my original idea to have a dinner date with Alex had been canceled. Scarlet must've heard it because she shot me a look.

"Shut up, you!" I demanded loudly at my noisy stomach.

"Girl, have you eaten today?" She demanded as the bartender handed me my card back, along with a receipt and a pen.

"Noooope. Fasssest-fastested-fasteded- you know what -*hic*- I'm trying to say. The easiest way to get -*hic*- wasted," I stated, a broad grin on my face, waving her off.

"Well, we're gonna go get something to eat. You want some pizza?" She offered, her face hopeful. Pizza sounded amazing. I grabbed the pen, moving my arms very broadly, and wrote out a twenty-dollar tip for the bartender. Or, at least, I tried to. My handwriting looked like a toddler had just scribbled all over the receipt. I scowled at it.

"Stupid pen. It drew aaaall over the place," I stated, blaming the innocent pen.

"Brina, give me the receipt. I'll write out the tip for you," Scarlet said, reaching over. I swung myself away, nearly toppling out of my seat before catching myself by grabbing the edge of the bar.

"Noooo! I wanna do it!" I whined, holding my receipt as far from her as I could manage.

"Girl! Do not make this more difficult than it needs to be," she said as she spun my stool around to face her, effectively snatching the pen and receipt from me. I pouted at her and crossed my arms. I slouched in my seat and started kicking my legs back and forth petulantly.

"There. Thank you, miss. Let's roll! Pizza awaits," Scarlet stated, as she grabbed my arm, half-leading, half-carrying me out of the bar. I perked up at the idea of a slice, forgetting why I was annoyed.

"Pizza? Yessss," I pumped my fist and got a small chuckle out of my friend.

"What am I gonna do with you?" She shook her head as she opened her passenger side door, helping me in and attempting to buckle me in, but I protested, preferring to do it myself.

"I got this!" I yelled, my annoyance making a return, as I drunkenly guided my seat belt into place, clicking it solidly closed. "Seeee?" I slurred, feeling accomplished, a grin returning to my face, which felt a little too warm.

"Oh yeah, you proved me wrong. Buckled up all by yourself. Good job," she said sarcastically. I chose to ignore her tone.

"Yes, I -*hic*- did." I nodded my head for emphasis, proud of myself.

Scarlet closed my door, and I immediately leaned my head against the window, letting the smooth glass cool my face. I was getting far too hot.

She got into the car and buckled herself in before starting it. She turned to me and asked me to stop leaning on the glass so she could roll the window down. I moved my head and leaned back against the headrest, relieved for the airflow as she did.

"Whatever you do, do not throw up in my car. I just got it detailed. Aim outside," she instructed.

"I'm not gonna throw up," I groaned as I felt my stomach growl once more. "I neeed piiizzaaaa."

"We'll see about that," Scarlet mumbled as she pulled away from the parking spot. I don't remember what happened next.

# 8

# I'm Fine

The world was way too fucking bright. I slowly opened my eyes and groaned at the familiar surroundings. I wasn't at home, but at Scarlet's place in her spare bedroom, recalling the red jacquard curtains I'd helped her pick out and hang up, and the black bedspread with silver ivy designs that were embossed onto it. My head pounded furiously, and my hand flew to cover my eyes, shielding me from the worst of the daylight that crept in through the blinds. The night before had been blanked from my memory. I knew we left the bar with Scarlet's promise of pizza, but everything after was gone. I needed answers, but first things first; I needed my head to stop pounding.

I slowly turned to face the left side of the bed, away from the wall the bed was pressed up against. There was a cup of water and two pills I knew to be Tylenol on the false oak side table, and I carefully consumed them, trying to minimize the pain of movement. I swallowed the last dregs of water, washing away the disgusting taste of bile. *Shit, I guess I wound up throwing up last night,* I thought. I lay back on the bed and threw the covers up over my eyes, determined to shield out the worst of the light. I just needed to wait out the worst of it.

There was a harsh rap of knuckles at the door, pounding hard, and a sharp pain jolted through my head. I groaned once again at the sudden assault of my senses.

"Go away," I mumbled into the pillow beneath me as I turned to bury my head into it.

The door opened, the sound of footsteps entered the room, and paused before a voice I recognized said, "It's about damn time you got up."

I peeked my eye out from under the covers and looked at a very irritated-looking Scarlet, her brows furrowed downward, and her hands on her hips.

"Did I throw up in your car?" I mumbled, still covered.

"Not the inside, but the outside of my passenger side door was covered. I had to take it to a car wash after I got you set up in here," she stated, arms folded across her chest.

"I feel like shit. What happened?" I asked, my mind brimming with questions.

She narrowed her eyes at me. "You don't remember? Well, I guess you wouldn't. Brina, you got me pulled over. I didn't get a ticket, but don't you remember going off on that cop?"

I blinked. I didn't remember shit.

Scarlet sighed and dropped her arms to her sides, walking over to sit on the bed with me, the sudden movement causing my head to nearly split open. I groaned in pain once again, pulling the covers over my head once more.

"You deserve that," she said pointedly. "What's the last thing you remember?"

I thought for a moment. I remembered leaving the bar after drinking a bunch within just a few minutes. Scarlet had promised pizza, I buckled my seat belt, she pulled out of the parking lot, and then nothing.

"I remember leaving the bar, but everything after that is a total dark spot," I said, slowly moving to sit up in the bed.

"Oh, that's it? Wow, lucky you. Do you know how impossible you are to rein in when you're drunk? You were so close to getting arrested and thrown in the drunk tank. Girl, you called an officer 'a pig ass motherfucker' for asking for your ID and then tried to get out of the car to fight him for telling you to watch yourself. I had to hold you back," Scarlet said with a look of annoyance.

"Why'd we get pulled over in the first place?"

Scarlet shifted her weight on the bed, looking uncomfortable.

"You grabbed the steering wheel. Brina, you almost made us swerve into another car. I don't know what was going through your head, but you almost got both of us killed."

The air was heavy with her admission. I hung my head, unable to make eye contact with her. Had I really done that? I wondered. I had a general distrust of the police, but damn. I'd never outright tried to fight an officer before. I must've had a good reason, but I knew that was not the time to speak that thought out loud.

"After he let us go, that's when you threw up. Then you laughed like it was the funniest shit ever. Seriously, you sounded unhinged. You joked that you'd made room for the pizza and tried to demand I go get us some. I was pissed at that point and almost drove you home for Alex to deal with. But I didn't. We picked up a pizza, got back to my place, and you passed out before you could eat a slice. I had to drag your ass to the bed and get you out of your dress. You're welcome for the pajamas, by the way," she added sardonically.

I removed the covers to find an oversized white nightgown where my fitted dress once was.

"Girl, what is with you? I told Alex you were staying the night, but he told me some things. Things that you've been doing recently. Impulse spending, picking fights, the D&D campaign, all of it. You don't have to lie to me. So please, answer me honestly, do you think you might be manic?" She forced eye contact, but I quickly looked away and rolled my eyes.

"Not you, too. Alex is paranoid. Don't let him get in your head," I grumbled.

"Brina-"

"If you're about to say it again, save it," I stated pointedly. "I'm not manic. I'm fine. Last night was stressful. I'm sorry for almost causing us to wreck, trying to fight an officer, and puking on your car. I'm sorry for all of it. But will you please stop trying to make it about my bipolar? Not everything has to do with me being bipolar." I looked at her expectantly.

Scarlet sighed, and her shoulders dropped as she looked away from me, her face a mask of disappointment. I felt my cheeks redden with annoyance. She was supposed to be on my side. She was my friend before she was Alex's. Why the hell was she backing up my husband?

"Look, I just want to go home. Can you drive me?" I asked, changing the subject.

"Alex is on his way. We need to have a talk. All three of us."

My heart skipped a beat, and all hints of annoyance vanished and were replaced by fury, the pain in my head temporarily forgotten. Were they trying to stage an intervention? Why? I was fine. It was one night of recklessness. I'd already apologized, and I had no plans of drinking like that again.

"So now I can't be trusted? What? Is that it?" I spat, not caring if my sudden shift in tone bothered my friend or not.

"What? Brina, no, it's not- I- We-" She stammered, eyes wide with surprise. Or fear. I couldn't tell which, but in that moment, it didn't matter to me.

I threw the covers off and stood up, leaving Scarlet tangled in them.

"Hey! Brina!" She exclaimed, pulling the covers off her head.

I narrowed my eyes at her.

"Do you think I'm fucking unstable or some shit?" I asked, vitriol coating each syllable.

"I didn't say that," she stated defensively.

"You didn't have to. If I were truly unstable, how would I still have it in me to keep my shit together when I have Luna? Answer me that." I crossed my arms and waited for her response. She stammered, but eventually she gave up trying to find an answer.

"Exactly. So I'm impulsive. I have ADHD. You know this, and Alex knows this. Luna has never, ever been in the car with me speeding. Not once. She's never seen me lose my shit. I know better than to act up around her. I'm a responsible parent, but you know what? Sometimes I just want to let loose. Not have to be 'Mommy' all the time. Not that you'd get that. You don't have any kids."

Scarlet was childfree by choice. Part of me envied her freedom, but I had never once regretted having Luna. She was a big reason for me to be the best version of myself. I was trying. Even her teacher commended mine and Alex's parenting the night before. That had to count for something.

I heard a car pull up outside the window. I knew the sound of those squeaky brakes. It was Alex. A renewed sense of anger and annoyance surged through me, my hangover long forgotten. He was there to try to control me. What was worse was that he had convinced Scarlet to do the same. I wasn't having it.

I grabbed my dress from the floor, where I guessed Scarlet had stripped me down to get changed, and pulled off my nightgown, not caring about my nudity bothering her. She'd already seen it all the night before when she changed me. I put my dress back on, found my shoes deposited in the corner of the room, and hurriedly pulled them on. I refused to sit through a fucking intervention. Why couldn't they tell last night was just a one-off incident? I was stressed from the fight with Alex and was doing my best to keep up with all my household and parental duties. They seriously needed to back off.

I quickly stormed out of the bedroom into the living room and right out the front door of the apartment, with Scarlet calling after me. I saw Alex getting out of the driver's side of the car and moved to the passenger door, opening the door and climbing in furiously. Glaring at him momentarily, I shifted my focus and looked straight ahead, my eyes fixed on the front door. Scarlet appeared outside and saw my husband looking dumbfounded. He closed the door and spoke to her, his back to me. I held out my arms in exasperation before dropping them. I could kind of hear their muffled voices, and my name stood out as they mentioned it a few times. They knew I hated being talked about like I wasn't there, but did it anyway.

As I sat there, watching them talk about me, I could've sworn I heard someone having an argument nearby that had nothing to do with Alex or Scarlet. I turned my head to look for the aggressor, but no matter which direction I looked in, I couldn't see anyone. For a moment, I thought the sun had dimmed, covered by a cloud or something. However, the sky was completely clear. The light returned to normal as quickly as it had shifted. *That was weird*, I thought, my anger temporarily forgotten.

# 9

# Audacity

While I was sitting in the car, waiting for something to change with Scarlet and Alex's discussion, I couldn't help but continue to look around, trying to find out where the argument was coming from. I couldn't quite make out what was being said, but I knew it wasn't kind. The people yelling sounded like two men screaming what I thought were profanities at each other. My gaze wandered away from my husband and friend as I looked out each window of the car, hoping to see whoever was yelling.

But there was nobody outside other than the two of them. The street behind the driveway was entirely clear. No cars were passing by, no people on the sidewalk, not even any birds chirping. There was absolutely nothing that would have indicated anyone was in the middle of an argument.

I caught Alex turn his head towards me out of the corner of my eye, his expression one of horror. What had Scarlet said to him? Why would he ever look at me like that? I was livid. I leaned over my seat towards the driver's side and smashed the horn violently, startling both my friend and husband.

"Let's go!" I yelled without rolling down the window, trying to hurry Alex along.

He gave me a stern look and stalked over to the driver's side door, opening it to lean his head inside.

"Don't honk my horn. Get out of the car. We need to talk. You, me, and Scarlet. She told me what you did last night," he asserted, his tone strict and unwavering.

I huffed at him, crossing my arms and refusing to move.

"Sabrina Marie, get out of the car now!" He bellowed, using my first and middle name. I hated when people did that.

"You can't make me," I stated harshly, refusing to move. "Take me home."

I saw something snap in Alex's eyes. He removed his head from inside the car, slammed his door shut, and furiously strode over to my door, forcefully opening it. He grabbed the buckle of my seat belt and undid it, grabbing my arm and yanking me out of the car so fast I hit my head on the roof.

"Ow! What the fuck?!" I screamed at him, my arms flying to my head.

"You got drunk, narrowly avoided a bar fight, tried to swerve Scarlet into another vehicle, and then almost got arrested!" He listed off angrily, ignoring that he caused me to hit my head. "What the fuck is wrong with you?! Do you have a death wish?!"

I was taken aback by his verbal assault. For the first time in weeks, I was speechless. I didn't have an answer for him. I didn't have a death wish, however. Quite the opposite. I'd never felt more alive. And there he was, screaming at me for having a wild night with my friend. Yeah, I saw his points, but it didn't mean I needed to validate them.

After a beat, I spoke again, my speech coming out rapidly, wanting to get this over with. "I don't have a death wish, and you know that. I fucked up. Sure, I got drunk, Alex. But people do stupid shit all the time when they're drunk. At least I'm still alive. So's Scarlet. Neither of us got hurt. Look, I won't do it again. Take all the alcohol out of the apartment if you want. I don't care. Whatever makes you feel the most secure."

His gaze didn't soften as I expected it to. Instead, he looked even angrier.

"The issue isn't the drinking. It's you. Whatever is going on in your head... this isn't the woman I married. You're being reckless. You're putting yourself and others in danger. You aren't sleeping, and I know you haven't been eating. There were no breakfast or lunch dishes in the sink on my day to do them. Can you explain all of that?" He asked, pointedly.

"So you're tracking me now? Monitoring me? Fuck, Alex, that's messed up! How would you feel if every move you made were scrutinized?" I demanded, defensively.

His face shifted from anger to frustration, his brow furrowed. "This isn't about me, and you know that. Why can't you see how much danger you put yourself in? How much you're neglecting yourself? Brina, for the love of everything, you could've died! Scarlet could've died."

"Could've but didn't. I just said I won't do it again! Back off, Alexander," I said icily.

"Oh shit," I heard from Scarlet, who was still standing on the porch of her apartment building. "Brina, I think you need to back off."

"Don't start with me! You told him everything and set this up. I thought you were my friend. But I guess not. Real friends don't rat on each other!" I yelled, pointing at her, my fury returning.

"Girl, you're not okay. Anyone can see that. I was just trying to get you help."

"I don't need help! I'm fine! Will everyone stop treating me like I'm some unstable maniac?! Fuck!" I screamed at the pair of them.

They shared a look before returning their gaze to me, faces of anger and concern mixed. I wasn't going to stand there and have my character slandered.

I turned on my heel and started walking away, not towards the car, but towards the sidewalk. Since I'd memorized the route to Scarlet's place from my own, I knew how to get back.

"Brina! Where the hell are you going?" Alex yelled.

"Home. One way or the other, I'm going home. If you won't take me, I'll walk!" I shouted back at him. There was an exasperated sigh, a quick apology to Scarlet, promising to update her later, before he headed down the driveway towards his car.

"Get in the car. We'll both go home." He stated through gritted teeth.

I turned back around and stalked towards the car. A dark satisfaction lingered in my mind, glad that I was able to get him to do exactly what I'd wanted in the first place. All I needed to raise enough hell to get him to do it.

As he climbed in and buckled himself, he made unrelenting eye contact with me, his gaze harsh, anger boiling just below the surface. I stared back at him, refusing to back down.

"Brina-" he started.

"Don't. I'm not in the mood to be accused of being reckless and irresponsible," I spat out, my speech faster than his.

"You- agh, forget it. I give up," Alex sighed as he started the engine, breaking eye contact, and pulled out of the driveway.

"What the hell is that supposed to mean?" I demanded, continuing to stare daggers at him.

"It means I'm so fed up with your shit. I need a break. So, I'm going to drop you off at home and go to my mother's for a while. Luna is coming with me," he said calmly in a voice that revealed just how exhausted he was. I knew Rebecca, his mother, would be fine with him staying with her, but I was not about to let him take our daughter away from me. That was absolutely unacceptable. I would not be separated from my child, no matter what.

"You are not taking Luna away from me. Don't even think about it," I hissed, my voice filled with undisguised fury.

"I don't think it's a good idea-"

"You don't think it's a good idea for her to be with her mother? Her mother, who has never once done anything to hurt her? That's what you think?" I interrupted angrily.

"Can you let me get a fucking word out?"

"I know what you're going to say. No point. Look, have I ever seemed like I would put Luna in danger, even when I was at my worst? Answer me honestly."

He sighed and ran a hand through his hair. He didn't have a counter to my direct question, just like I knew he wouldn't.

"Brina, this isn't like other times-"

"Bullshit, it isn't! Name one damn time I've ever, ever put her in danger."

"You're acting impulsively. You said so yourself. I'm just worried about Luna."

"What? Because I'm so fucking dangerous? When did you become such a stiff? You said I'm not the woman you married, but you aren't the man I married either. The man I married would trust me with our daughter because I would never hurt her."

Alex looked over at me with icy contempt. He spoke his next words through gritted teeth.

"Fine. You'd better update me every hour on her until her bedtime. I swear on everything I love, if you do anything that could even remotely hurt Luna... well, I don't know what I'd do, but it won't be pretty," he finished.

I rolled my eyes but ultimately conceded. I'd do whatever it took to keep my daughter with me, where she belonged.

We arrived home after driving in silence for a few minutes. I got out of the car quickly and made a beeline for the door, Alex not far behind me.

"I thought you were just going to drop me off," I stated once I'd unlocked the door and headed inside.

"Yeah, and I need to pack a bag for a few days. I'll be quick. Don't forget to pick up Luna from the bus stop," he said curtly.

I went to sit down in the living room, giving myself space from my husband. I needed it, or I was going to lose my shit again. He made his way to our bedroom, and I could hear him opening drawers, most likely stuffing clothes into his green suitcase that I'd gifted him for our anniversary last year, when I surprised him with a vacation for the three of us, me, him, and Luna.

I had budgeted and pulled excess money from our checking account, meticulously calculating how much we would need and what we could realistically afford to put back each month. I'd planned it for so long, carefully got Alex's boss's number from his phone, and requested the time off for it, as he never used his vacation days that year. He was so thrilled and relieved that I'd planned everything out for him. We spent a week in a four-star hotel and enjoyed being together, going out to lunches and dinners that I'd researched and budgeted for. A lot of time was spent at the indoor pool, which the hotel included for its guests' use. It was such a great vacation. I wondered if things would ever be that good again as he appeared from the room and left through the front door, not uttering a single word to me.

# 10

# Freedom

With Alex gone, the apartment was strangely quiet. I had an hour or two before I had to pick up Luna. My skull buzzed with excess energy from my fight with Alex and confrontation with Scarlet. Looking around, I saw my home had gotten a little messy since my night out. There was a bowl lying out, some blankets and pillows thrown sloppily on the couch, and some of Luna's toys were scattered about the floor. Nothing a quick pickup couldn't fix.

I got to work, effectively distracting myself from the commotion of earlier, but I was done within just a few minutes, leaving me with my racing thoughts once again. *How could they treat me like that? Like I was a child who needed constant monitoring. Didn't they understand I regretted last night? I promised not to do any of that again, and I intend to stick to my word. Why am I the only one who sees that I'm fine?* I wondered. Sure, I'd put myself and Scarlet in danger. I felt truly terrible for that, but neither of us got hurt. That had to count for something, right?

I started pacing around my home furiously, muttering to myself about how nobody got me. Out of the corner of my eye, I could've sworn I saw a person standing in my hallway. I zoomed around to get a better look, worried that someone had gotten into my house without me noticing. There was nobody there. *What the hell is going on? Did they run and hide?*

I started searching for the person I thought I saw cloaked in shadows, and I could've sworn I saw something move around me. Like a shadow running across the bottom of the wall. I spun around, trying to get a better glimpse of whatever was tormenting me.

"Stop hiding! Show yourself!" I yelled. There was no response. I continued searching for the shadow person, but to no avail.

*Whatever. It was probably just a trick of the light. Most likely, it was my own shadow that startled me. Yeah, that's it,* I decided. I pulled out my phone, thinking I'd just felt it buzz, but there was no notification. Weird. At least it gave me a chance to check the time. I had about fifteen minutes until I had to pick up Luna. *How did I lose so much time? How long was the shadow person picking on me?* I wondered, slightly panicked.

I quickly changed from my dress that I had worn the day before into a crop top and shorts, feeling a bit hot from all the running around, looking for the shadow. As I headed out the door to wait at the bus stop for my daughter, I was assaulted by the too-bright light of day. I covered my eyes, waiting for them to adjust to the light, but they simply wouldn't. I went back inside the apartment to grab a pair of sunglasses off the table that was near the entryway and put them on, not willing to be blinded again.

The world outside seemed to have dimmed some since I put on the glasses. I slowly raised them to sit on top of my head and found the sunlight tolerable. No longer blinding. *What was up with that?* I wondered as I walked down the block to stand at the corner and wait for the big yellow bus. I tapped my foot impatiently, willing the bus to hurry up and get there.

When I heard the recognizable engine, my head swung around, excited to greet my little girl. It pulled up ever so slowly, and I groaned while I waited for it to stop and let Luna out. The bus had finally stopped and opened its doors, allowing several children off before my daughter's chestnut hair appeared at the open door.

I held out my arms, prepared to give her a big hug, but she simply walked up to me and asked what I was doing.

"I just wanted to give you a hug, Baby," I replied, putting my arms down as she walked past me towards the apartment building. That was pretty normal for her. She didn't always respond to me or others when we spoke. I followed her, and soon we were home. It was time for me to text Alex, letting him know

I got Luna.

I whipped out my phone from my pocket and quickly texted Alex, *'She's home, safe and sound,'* before tucking it away just as quickly. I wanted to make today fun for Luna, at least until it was time for her to go to bed.

"Luna, what do you want for dinner? I'm gonna make whatever you'd like," I beamed at her.

She paused for a minute, tapping her tiny finger to her chin, deep in thought. A sudden smile spread across her face before she bellowed, "Ice cream! Chocolate and ice cream, please, Mommy!" I laughed at her adorably predictable response and turned towards the kitchen, prepared to make her a huge ice cream Sunday with chocolate sprinkles on top. Just the way I knew she liked it. I could indulge her today. Who cared what anyone else thought? It was just one day.

The day quickly became evening; I indulged every whim of Luna's, from ice cream and chocolate sprinkles to playing dress up, complete with her playing in my makeup, not caring how much she destroyed it because she was having fun. Who cared if it was expensive? I'd simply buy more later. My daughter's happiness was all that I wanted. I had remembered to text Alex roughly every hour, only to be met with silence on his end. I saw the green check mark in the messages, showing he'd seen the message. Luckily, he wasn't replying, so I didn't have to deal with him.

After hours of playing, I still had the energy to spend, but Luna was getting crankier and crankier, testing my patience. I looked at my phone to check the time, wondering if she might've been tired, and saw it was nearly 45 minutes past her bedtime.

"Shit," I said simply.

"Bad word, Mommy!" Luna stomped her foot at me. I rolled my eyes at her, annoyed that she called me out.

"Luna, chill. I'm a grownup. I can say whatever I want. It's time for bed," I stated swiftly.

"No! No bedtime!" She screamed.

"Hey! Don't yell at me. Now, go brush your teeth, go potty and get to bed. It's not up for debate, Missy. You've got school tomorrow," I scolded sternly, not appreciating getting yelled at by yet another person that day.

Luna stomped off to the bathroom and I heard the sink turn on aggressively. I sighed and rubbed my temples. That kid was testing my limits. The toilet flushed and she emerged from the bathroom, walking right past me and slamming her bedroom door shut.

"Watch the attitude!" I hollered after her. At least she was in bed. I was free for the night. I could do whatever I wanted. What was I going to do since I had so much free time? I certainly wasn't going to waste my energy on sleep; that was for sure.

Maybe I could text my younger sister, Abigail. It had been a bit since we'd last talked. I hadn't heard from her or our other younger sister, Zoe, in a few weeks. It'd be nice to catch up with them.

I got my phone out of my pocket and went to my messages. Still nothing from Alex, which was absolutely fine by me. He was being a real thorn in my side lately. I quickly typed out that Luna was in bed and that everything was alright. Quickly exiting that chat, I scrolled through my logs and found mine and Abigail's thread. I opened it and typed out 'Hey Sissy. You busy? I've got piping hot tea to spill.'

Not even a minute passed before she saw the message, as indicated by a green check mark at the bottom right of the page. She started typing, three grey dots bouncing up and down. I waited for her reply impatiently, growing annoyed at how slowly she typed. After a moment, there was a new message from her.

'Yeah, I'm busy rebuilding the Empire State Building from scratch. What's up?' It read.

I laughed at her sarcasm. Between the three of us siblings, she had always been the most feceious. I quickly hit the call button on the message thread, and the phone rang for a few moments before my sister answered.

"Bitch, when I said what's up, that didn't mean you could call me. How dare you? The audacity!" She joked dramatically. I giggled at that.

"Oh, please, you're full of audacity. Constantly. I have updates for you. Alex is being such an ass. He stormed out and is sleeping at his mother's because of a misunderstanding. He's blowing things out of proportion and-" I started rapidly.

"Whoa, slow down! I can't understand a word you're saying. Alex did what now?"

I felt my jaw twinge in annoyance. Why was everyone trying to slow me down? I was so sick of it.

"No, you need to speed up." I quipped. "Keep up with me here. I was out drinking with Scarlet and-"

"Brina, I can't. What's with you? So fucking snippy," she pointed out. That was it. I couldn't deal with her judging me, too.

"You know what? Never mind. You're being a judgmental ass, just like everyone else!"

"What? Brina I-"

I hung up before she could finish her sentence, throwing my phone at the couch. It bounced off and fell on the floor.

"Mother fucker!" I yelled, thinking the screen had just cracked. Stupid fragile glass. I quickly picked it up, checking for damage. Luckily, there was only a small crack on the top left corner where it hit the floor. Thank goodness for minimal damage.

I released a sigh of annoyance, pacing around the living room once again, my thoughts speeding up even faster. *Damned Abigail. Damned Alex. Scarlet, too. Everyone was against me. They were all probably in cahoots. Trying to convince me I'm losing it. I'm not. I'm perfectly stable! Why couldn't they see that? So what if I had more energy than normal? I used that energy to do things for them. Like the D&D campaign. Alex would've loved that. But you know what? Who cares what he would've liked?*

I moved quickly to my laptop and opened the file I had saved for the campaign. I selected every file swiftly, mis-clicking a few times, fueling my rage, before I finally hit 'delete'. I exited the files, leaving only the main file labeled simply 'Alex D&D' as an empty shell. The trashcan icon was on the left side of the laptop; I emptied it. The campaign was gone. The hours and days I had spent creating it, all down the drain. But I didn't care. It would teach Alex a lesson. He couldn't treat me like I was crazy and expect the good stuff from me.

I didn't feel satisfied, but instead found my annoyance and anger growing. I needed a dab.

The concentrate was in the bathroom, locked up high on a shelf above where Luna, or I for the matter, couldn't reach. I had to grab a step stool to get it. I grabbed the small glass container out of the shoebox and my dab rig. The blowtorch was behind the box, as it didn't fit inside it. It was a small handheld, but industrially intended, torch. I stepped off the stool and put it back under the bathroom cabinet. I set up the concentrate in the small glass container and clicked off the safety on the blowtorch. Adjusting the dial, I moved it from low to medium flame, making sure it'd get hot enough to properly heat the nail of the rig. I positioned the dab rig out in front of me, pushed the button of the torch with my thumb, and proceeded to heat it until it was glowing red. Quickly releasing my thumb from the button, I put the torch down and angled the rig just right to tap the concentrate in the glass, creating smoke that I immediately inhaled.

I held my breath, containing the cannabis smoke in my lungs, before releasing it and coughing up a storm. I had taken an absolutely massive hit. A wave of nausea threatened to overwhelm me, and I leapt for the toilet, just in case. I held my head over the bowl, feeling the nausea eventually ebb and fade completely.

My head was buzzing with the high I'd obtained. Suddenly, things didn't feel that bad anymore. I lifted my head from the toilet and looked at the mirror above the sink. My reflection stared back at me, eyes red and lids hooded. Yep, I was definitely stoned. I couldn't have hidden it from anyone if they saw me. Something about this made me smile and laugh. I laughed harder than I had in my entire life. Beside me, the shadow figure had made a reappearance, and he brought friends, all dancing around. I laughed at their ridiculous attempt to hide from me. To stay out of the center of my vision. Maybe they were scared of me, just like I thought Alex was. How he thought I was unstable. Well, I was going to prove him wrong, then and there.

Still laughing, I grabbed the blowtorch from the counter and started swinging it above my head rapidly. I'd finally caught one of the shadows that had gotten closer to my center of vision and pointed the torch at it. It tried to run, but I blasted the torch at it, my thumb pressed down hard. The shadow figure narrowly missed getting hit by my flame. I laughed at it again.

"What, are you afraid of me? Am I that scary?" I started, cackling maniacally. I took aim at another shadow that dared to make itself known to me and clicked the button of the torch on and off rapidly in its direction. "You scared I'm gonna burn you? Ha ha ha!" I felt amazing. So amazing, I felt like I was going to split at the seams, my smile nearly as wide as my pupils, I noticed, looking back at the mirror. I laughed once more.

"You have no idea how good I feel! No fucking idea at all! Ha ha ha! Nobody can ever meet me on my level. Never! Hahahaha!" I exclaimed, still swinging the torch around, clicking it on and off above my head, nearly scorching the shower curtain, but I readjusted to aim at another shadow that was trying really hard to run away from me. I thought I heard it let out a muffled scream, but I just guffawed at it and hollered, "Don't be a wuss!" as I clicked the flame on once again, but I missed. The shadow had gotten away. There were still more, all dancing around me, and I aimed at each and every one of them, giggling as I did, blasting the torch multiple times.

I got an idea in my head. I looked at the blowtorch in my hand, still laughing like mad, and slowly turned it towards my face, finding it absolutely hilarious. *If I were so unstable, could I do this?* I thought, as I slowly moved the torch closer and closer to my head, stopping about an inch away from my temple, thumb poised on the button, ready to press it at any moment.

I applied gentle pressure, heard the hiss of the butane, and laughed before releasing it slightly and pressing again, making it hiss once more. I found this hysterical and dropped my arms to my sides, torch in hand. Tears of laughter blurred my vision. I put the torch down inside the cabinet with the stool, along with the dab rig and concentrate container, not caring if they were stored back up on the shelf or not. That was Alex's rule, not mine. So I naturally had to break it.

I was about to leave the bathroom, feeling on top of the world. I was still laughing like a crazy person, but then I saw it. Something so faint, I could've probably been imagining it, but I was sure I wasn't. A small scorch mark on the wall by the mirror. Barely an inch big, mainly just soot that could be wiped away easily, but it was definitely there. I swiped at it, confirming what I'd thought, as it covered my thumb.

"Wait, that could've gone very wrong." I looked in the mirror, my eyes still red, but my head clear suddenly, the high from before forgotten.

"This isn't normal," I realized. I needed help. Right then, or else I didn't know what more .I'd do. I quickly left the bathroom and ran to the living room, shaky hands reaching for my phone. I unlocked it swiftly and pulled up Alex's text thread. I sent him three simple words: '*I need help.*'

I waited for his reply, but there wasn't even a green check mark to tell me he'd seen my message. I groaned and sat on the couch, determined to sit there and not mess with anything else until he got back to me. I'd really messed up that time. And now the one person I always thought I could count on was ignoring me. I sat for hours, seeing the dim light of day start to creep through the windows, before I finally crashed on the couch, having given up on Alex responding to me. What was I going to do?

# 11

# I Need Help

I was awoken by Alex shaking my arm roughly, his face etched with worry.

"Brina? Are you okay?" His eyes searched mine for an answer.

I blinked away the grogginess I felt, groaning as I sat up on the couch. I looked at my husband helplessly and shook my head.

"You were right. I'm manic. Was manic. I don't know," I admitted, not knowing exactly how I felt. All I knew was that I felt drained. Physically, mentally, and in every other way I could barely think of.

Alex opened his mouth to say something, his face weary, before I heard Luna's door click open. We both looked in that direction before our eyes met again.

"Go lie down in the bedroom. I'm going to get Luna ready and take her to school. I'll be back as soon as I can," he instructed, his voice calm, but full of authority. I gave him a long look, wishing I could have him just hold me in his arms, but ultimately complied.

I entered the bedroom and flopped down hard on the bed, exhausted. I didn't mean to, but I dozed off again, waiting for Alex to drop off Luna. It felt like no time had passed, and I was awoken by Alex once again, looking concerned.

"What happened? I'm so sorry I didn't see your text when you sent it. I was asleep. I went to bed after you told me Luna went down, which was about an hour after she was supposed to, by the way," he added sternly.

"I know. I'm sorry. I completely lost track of time. It's not an excuse, I know, but I did and I regret it," I admitted, my head hung low, hiding behind my dark black hair.

"You-you're sorry?" He said, sounding astonished.

"Yes. I am. I'm so sorry, Honey. I've been such an asshole to everyone, Luna included. I don't expect you to forgive me-" I started, but Alex interrupted me by pulling me into his arms, holding me right there on the bed, my head pinned to his chest.

"I forgive you, Hun. I knew something was wrong. You weren't yourself. I knew that, but it didn't make it any easier."

"I know. I wish I could go back and fix it all. Things had gotten so bad, I was seeing shadows and hearing people arguing," I mumbled into his chest.

"You were having hallucinations?" He asked, moving slightly to look down at me, worry clear on his face.

"Yeah," I answered quickly, hiding my face on his chest once more.

We sat like that for a long while, forgetting the world around us existed. I was the first to break contact, feeling overwhelmed by everything that happened, feeling like I didn't deserve his comfort. Alex looked me over, assessing me, checking for something I couldn't identify. He saw my arm, and saw a purple bruise present from the night at the bar, where I'd hit it. He avoided the area but looked at me with gentle concern, lifting my arm to check me over.

"Physically, I'm fine." I pulled my arm away from him carefully, not feeling any pain. "But Alex, things got so intense last night. I did a large dab, and then I started playing with the blowtorch, swinging it around and blasting it. I-" I hesitated. I didn't want to cause Alex any more worry than he likely already felt. His eyes were locked on mine, not wavering.

"Go on. Tell me what happened," he said, waiting patiently. I took a steadying breath and spoke.

"I pointed the torch at myself and almost pushed the button," I finished, unable to look at him.

"Oh my God. Brina... I don't- I mean, why would you do something so reckless?" He stammered, shocked by my admission. I didn't mention the shadow people I saw during the episode, thinking that would have overwhelmed him completely. I felt it was enough that I'd already mentioned them moments ago. "Were you seeing things then?"

"No, I was just pretending that I was in a group of people, thinking I was scaring them," I half-lied, trying to spare him that particular detail. "I thought it was all so funny. I couldn't stop laughing, but it was so terrifying right after, when I thought about how I could've burned myself so badly, or worse," I got out, my head still low, not meeting his gaze.

"Oh, Hun. I'm so sorry I wasn't here for you. I should've stayed. I should've..." He trailed off.

"Don't blame yourself, this is all me. Alex, I think I need professional help. I need to get back on meds or something. Movement disorder be damned," I stated, finally looking up. His hands were in his hair, and his focus was on the wall next to him.

"You're right. You need help. Come on. I'll drive you to the hospital. They should be able to get you on something that'll help," he said, standing and offering me his hand.

I thought for a moment. If I told a professional what had just happened, there was no way I'd be returning home the same day. I didn't want to get put away, especially since Luna's birthday was coming up that weekend, just days away.

"Alex, if I go to the hospital and tell them what happened, they're gonna admit me. I know it," I stated as calmly as I could muster, my voice cracking at the word 'admit'.

"You don't know that for sure. They could probably just give you some meds to balance you out and send you home," he replied, naively.

I sighed. It was going to happen. I just knew it, but how was Alex going to take it when he found out for sure?

"If I'm admitted, ask your mother for help with Luna."

"You're not going to get admitted, Brina. Are you still manic?"

I shrugged. I really didn't know how I felt, but I knew I was out of the energy I had the night before.

He sighed and stood up from the bed.

"Come on. Let's go get your hair and teeth brushed. I'll take you to the hospital right after."

I took his still outstretched hand and moved with slow, short steps, not wanting to go to the hospital, but knowing it was inevitable. I needed to get help so I could be the best possible version of myself for Luna and Alex.

We made it to the bathroom, where Alex grabbed the hairbrush and started brushing my hair as I brushed my teeth. It felt nice to have someone do that for me. Once we were done, it was time to go.

Alex stood at the front door, opening it, revealing the light of day. He held out a hand and offered me the saddest smile in the world.

"Ready?" He asked.

"No, but I'm gonna do it anyway."

# Epilogue

The drive to the hospital felt both incredibly fast and slow simultaneously. The dead leaves of autumn blew by us as Alex drove cautiously ahead. At first, we didn't speak. I didn't know what to say. I knew what was awaiting me when we got to the hospital. They'd admit me. I'd be locked away. I was terrified of missing Luna's birthday party that upcoming Sunday. It was Thursday and I knew, because I pointed that blowtorch at myself, they'd keep me at for 72 hours at least. I leaned my head against the cold glass of the window and sighed, watching my breath fog it up.

"You know I don't blame you for any of this, right?" Alex asked out of the blue.

I looked over at him. His eyes were glued to the road ahead, his brows raised, waiting for a reply.

"I would," I grumbled, still feeling ashamed of myself for putting him through so much. All he had ever done was try to help me and keep our family safe. He was never trying to control me.

"Brina, be lenient with yourself. You were manic. It wasn't your fault."

"Is it too late to turn around?" I asked, terrified about the certain reality that I had ahead of me.

"Yes," he said without missing a beat. "Look, you didn't actually hurt anybody. I really think they'll help you adjust your meds, and we should be good to go."

"That's delusional thinking, Alex. They're going to admit me. I pointed something dangerous at myself."

"You're calling me delusional? Who's the one who's been seeing shit?" He joked. It didn't land for me. I looked away from him, hurt that he used my recent hallucinations against me. There was a sharp inhale from him as he realized what he had said. "Sorry. Too soon."

"I mean, if you're already willing to joke about it..." I started, trying to see the humor in all that had occurred. "I really suck at regulating my emotions, don't I?" I said flatly, unable to force a sarcastic tone.

"Yeah, you do, but it was so much more than that, wasn't it?"

"Stupid chemical misfires," I mumbled, trying to find something funny about that situation.

Alex chuckled slightly.

"That sounds more like the woman I married. Making light of things," he said, removing his right hand from the steering wheel to hold my left, his thumb rubbing the gold wedding band on my ring finger.

"If I can't laugh and make fun of things, then I'd probably cry. If I could," I pointed out, having been unable to since the phone call with my father. Maybe that had to do with the mania. Who knew?

We were only a few blocks away from the hospital. I looked over at my husband and studied his every feature as if it were the last time I was going to get to see him. I noticed how the sun lit up his chestnut hair, illuminating it with a touch of red. His blue eyes were bright, but filled with a sadness he couldn't quite keep hidden from me.

"I really am sorry for everything I've put you through. What I put Luna through. All of it," I reiterated, feeling awful for the way I had been for the last month.

"You don't need to apologize, my love. I'm not angry. Everything that happened, I mean, it's a lot to process, you know?" He said without taking his eyes off the road, coming to a stop in the hospital parking lot.

"Do I ever," I stated. I looked outside. The sky was a dull, dismal grey. What a perfect day to get admitted to the psych ward. I didn't get out of the car. Alex killed the engine and turned to look at me.

"Regardless of whatever happens today, I'm not going anywhere. You've got me. Always. You're stuck with me just like I'm stuck with you," he said sadly.

"So you're stuck with me?" I teased lightly.

"And you with me," he replied.

## EPILOGUE

"Okay. Let's go in. I'm as ready as I'll ever be," I said, unbuckling myself and stepping out of the car into the hospital. We walked together, his hand on my back, offering me comfort. As we entered the crowded waiting area, Alex approached the person at the front desk.

"My wife needs a mental health evaluation."

# Afterword

Congratulations! You've reached the end of the story. That was a wild ride, wasn't it? Brina really put everyone through the wringer, including herself. But this is far too often the reality of someone living with Bipolar Disorder. I, Brittany, the author of this book, know this all too well. Unfortunately, from personal experience. I hope that this story helps to spread awareness about living with bipolar and what to look out for in either yourself or loved ones with the diagnosis. If you ever find yourself in crisis, please, reach out to your loved ones and your area's crisis hotline. Below is the information to reach the national Suicide and Crisis Hotlines in both the United States and Canada. Thank you for reading, and you can catch the immediate aftermath of Brina's crisis in my debut novel, When the Flame Goes Out.

US- Call or Text 988 for the Suicide & Crisis Hotline

Canada- Call or Text 988 for the Suicide Crisis Hotline

## About the Author

Brittany L.J. Roberts is the author of the debut novel, When the Flame Goes Out. She returns to Brina's world with the novella, Catching a Match—a short, intense prequel that explores the chaotic, escalating moments of Brina's mania, detailing the critical events that precede her time in the behavioral health unit. Brittany is dedicated to sharing honest, nuanced stories of mental health, vulnerability, and the journey toward recovery.

**You can connect with me on:**
- https://bljroberts-author.com
- https://www.facebook.com/BrittanyLJRobertsauthor

# Also by Brittany L.J. Roberts

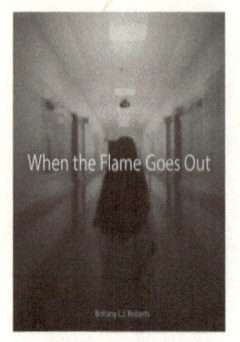

**When the Flame Goes Out**

Brina is fighting to get better. With a pre-existing bipolar diagnosis, she thought she could manage her mental health by pouring energy into creative projects instead of seeking help. Now, after a severe manic episode, she's trapped inside a behavioral health unit.

In a world where nurses and techs stay behind a locked door, Brina's own mind feels like a cage. Her thoughts race, she's disoriented and confused, and her biggest fear is staying inside longer than she needs to. Her freedom hinges on every reaction, and every day is a test.

Brina wants to get back home, back to normal, to be a better wife and a better mom for her daughter. But what if "getting better" isn't for them? What if it's for herself? The stakes couldn't be higher: if she can't find a way to heal, she risks losing the family she's fighting so hard to keep.

www.ingramcontent.com/pod-product-compliance
Lightning Source LLC
LaVergne TN
LVHW041625070526
838199LV00052B/3246